The Heartbreaker

NEW YORK TIMES BESTSELLING AUTHOR

CLAIRE CONTRERAS

The Heartbreaker

Prologue

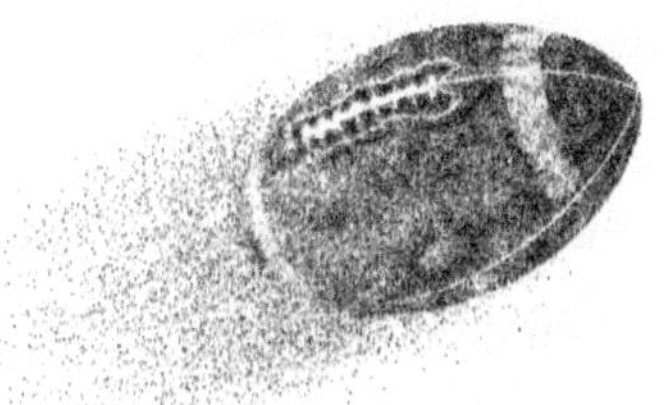

4 Years Ago

I WALK INTO THE FRAT HOUSE WITH MY FRIEND AND TEAMMATE, JILL, at my side. My heart is beating so fast I can barely stand it. I don't know why I'm so nervous. I've been to a college party before, just not when I was actually in college. I look around, unable to take the smile off my face.

"I'm going to the bathroom. Meet me in the kitchen?" Jill says.

"Sure." I start walking in the direction where I assume the kitchen is and come to a full stop just before I get there.

There are a lot of guys in there. A lot. Like too many for me to just waltz in and be all cool without also being insanely awkward. One simply cannot be both, and it is a choice we make. Like right now, if I decide that I am cooler than I am, no one will think to question it. I know this because I've studied the art of cool from effortlessly cool people. Still, as I stand there, palms sweaty, I feel like I may need ten more minutes to give myself this pep talk. One of the guys laughs loudly, throwing his head back with it. He's blond and has a summer vacation tan, with a pink neck and cheeks. He's hot. Like really hot. In front of him, with his back facing me, is a guy with impeccable crisped golden skin. He's wearing a black t-shirt, jeans, and a blacked-out Yankees ball cap that faces my direction, strands of his longish hair tucked beneath it. Blondie may be hot as hell, but he has nothing on this guy. I haven't even seen his face, and I already know it. Then, he turns around as if feeling my eyes on him. He's mid-sentence, his straight white teeth showing as he speaks, and then he completely stops talking, and my heart completely stops beating when those toffee-colored eyes hit mine.

"Josephine?" He frowns, then smiles. "Josephine! Holy shit."

Jagger Cruz.

Holy shit.

Jagger Cruz, who's cool in an effortless, I own-my-shit kind of way. He's always been hot, but now that he's grown into his skin, he's . . . beyond.

"I didn't know you were here," I say stupidly. "I mean, mom mentioned you were coming to UNC like Mitch, but I didn't know you were here already."

"Yeah. I went by the house the other day, but you weren't there." He's grinning, eyeing me up and down, openly checking me out. My skin prickles. This is entirely too nerve-racking for me.

"I live on campus," I say. "With a roommate."

"Ah, I thought you'd stay at home since you're so close."

"I want the college experience." I smile.

"I hear that." He glances around, says bye to some of the guys he was talking to as they pass by, and fist bumps him.

"You're not going to introduce me to your friend?" Blondie looks at me, then at Jagger, whose perfect jaw twitches just a bit but manages to smile at his friend.

"Sure. Josephine, this is Lawrence. Lawrence, this is Josephine."

"Hi." I smile, feeling my cheeks turn pinker than they already are. He looks like an Abercrombie model. They both do.

"Josephine. I like that." Lawrence winks. "I hope to see you around."

"Uh, yeah. Sure. Me too." I wave as he walks away and looks back at Jagger. "College parties, am I right?"

"Right." He's quiet for a moment, his eyes assessing me. "You want a drink?"

"Sure." I shrug a shoulder and follow him.

"What's your poison?" He glances over at me when we make it to a foldable table with many bottles on it.

"I think I'll go with the tequila."

"Tequila." He raises an eyebrow. "Ballsy."

"It's the only thing that doesn't give me a massive hangover."

"Said no one ever," he says with a chuckle that hits me right in the chest.

He starts pouring it for me the way I tell him I want it—on the rocks, with a wedge of lime. Fancy shit for a college party, but this is only my second college party, so I haven't gotten the memo on what to drink. Also, I barely drink, so I'm just having what my dad normally has. Lame. So lame, but I can't exactly act like I don't know what I'm doing in front of Jagger Cruz, who always seems to know what he's doing.

"Hey, Jagger," a girl says, smiling as she walks over with two friends in tow.

"Hey," he says, grinning at her as he finishes pouring our drinks and hands mine over to me.

I thank him and fish out my phone to check on Jill while he talks to the group of girls. They're cheerleaders, and since he's on the football team, they have a lot to talk about.

Me: where are you?

Jill: in the living room. Talking to Reid. Where are you? I saw you with a hot guy and didn't want to cock block

Me: I just got a drink

Jill: With the hot guy?

Me: he's a family friend, and yes

Jill: *fire emoji*

Me: LOL

Jill: I'm going to hang out with Reid unless you want company

Me: I'm good

Jill: Check in with you in an hour?

Me: Ok

I put my phone away and look up as I sip my tequila. I would join the conversation, but honestly, I don't want to and the girls haven't so much as glanced at me.

"Text me," the original one says, winking at Jagger as she walks away.

Jagger doesn't say anything. He just turns back to me.

"Such a ladies' man," I say.

"A gift and a curse." He sips his drink. "How's your drink?"

"Strong."

"Well, you did request tequila on the rocks."

"It's good, though. Refreshing."

"Hm."

"What are you drinking?"

"Same thing as you." He shrugs. "I figured I should try it."

"And?"

"It's all right."

"Just all right?" I laugh.

"I'm not much of a drinker, so I feel like this is going to knock me on my ass."

"Same." I take another sip.

"I never thought I'd see the day Josephine Canó would be trying to get drunk at a party."

"I guess . . . I guess I figure it'll help give me a little bit of courage, you know?"

"Courage for what?"

"To talk to guys and stuff."

He chuckles, shaking his head. "Every guy who's walked by has checked you out. I don't think you need any kind of courage."

"They haven't talked to me." I feel myself frown.

"Because you're with me." He winks. "I've been giving off she's mine vibe."

"Oh." My heart slams into my chest. I swallow. "Do you

. . . " I pause and lick my lips. "Do you want me to be yours? For the night, I mean."

"Are you offering?"

"Maybe." I take another sip of the tequila.

Jagger grins. It's a slow grin that transforms his already gorgeous face into something even hotter, and suddenly, I feel like there isn't enough air in this room.

"So, what are you studying?" he asks after a moment.

"Public Health."

"Nice."

"Nice or boring?" I bite my lip, and when his eyes drop to my mouth, I feel myself blush furiously. "Your mouth is saying nice, but your eyes are saying boring."

"Nothing about you is boring." His gaze darkens as he says the words and takes a step forward.

I'm well aware that we're in a loud, crowded party, but at this moment, when Jagger is looking at me like he wants to devour me, it's as if the world disappears. For so long, too long, I've been Good Girl Josephine. The one who doesn't go home past curfew and doesn't date the wrong boy. My sister, who's only a year younger than me, has always tried to get me to rebel a little, and while I cover for her when she decides to stay out later, it's just not in me to push buttons.

I take a deep breath and then another and do something I've only dreamed of. I take one step closer to Jagger, watching the way his gaze blazes as I put a hand on his hard chest and kiss him. It's a quick kiss. A peck. Jagger blinks, surprised when I pull away. His eyes search mine for a moment, just long enough to convince himself of what to do next. He takes our cups, sets them down, and grabs my hand, leading me to the back of the room and then up the stairs. Once we're there, standing in the hall, where there are doors open and closed, and the music is still loud but not as loud as downstairs, he turns to me. My heart is beating so hard, so fast, I'm not sure what to do with it.

"I thought it would be quieter up here," he says after a moment, glancing toward the stairs. "I guess not."

"And here I was thinking you were leading me to a bedroom." I tilt my head slightly. Jagger's eyes widen as he looks at me again.

"Do you want me to lead you to a bedroom?"

"I wouldn't have followed you up here if I didn't."

He grazes his lower lip with his perfect teeth as he studies me, and my heart flips. Even though I grew up around him, seeing him tonight feels like meeting him for the first time. Maybe it's the ambiance or the fact that our parents and siblings aren't sitting steps away from us for the first time. Maybe it's that while I have always been attracted to him, I've never been as attracted to him as I am at this moment. Whatever the case, I vow to let tonight goes wherever my body wants it to go. I'm not going to talk myself out of anything. I'm not going to reprimand myself for being too forward.

"My offer stands, you know," I say, "About being yours for the night."

"Jesus." He huffs out a laugh, raking a hand through his perfect, thick waves.

For a moment, I'm not sure what to think, and I settle on

the insecurity that maybe I came off too strong and he doesn't know how to let me down easily. Or maybe he thinks this is crazy since our families go way back. My thoughts come to a halt when he takes a step closer to me. He brings a hand up and clasps the back of my neck, pulling me toward him. My heart stops beating as our lips meet in the softest kiss. My lips part when his tongue touches the seam of my mouth and I gasp against him when it meets my tongue, dancing to a beat of a sensual song I've never quite felt before. His hand cups my breast over my shirt and I groan, feeling that action between my legs. I pull away, breaking the kiss, vision spotty as I look up at him.

"Do you . . . can we go to a room?"

He bites his lip and pulls me into the room behind him, shutting the door and locking it. It's a guy's room, but the bed is perfectly made, and it looks more organized than my room has ever been. It's weird and surprising. He lets me look around for a second before he's on me again, his lips on my neck, sucking as he explores. I shut my eyes and throw my head back, gripping his t-shirt tightly for a second before tucking my hands underneath his shirt and running my fingers along with his rock-hard abs. He brings his mouth to mine again and kisses me like he's dreamed of this moment. I wonder, for a moment, if I should tell him that I'm a virgin. I decide against it. It's not like I have an STD that I need to disclose. On that note, when he pulls back from the kiss and begins to undress me, I shut my brain off and go with it.

Chapter One

JOSEPHINE." MY FATHER'S VOICE ROARS THROUGH HIS PRIVATE practice.

"Uh-oh," Donna says, shooting me a sympathetic glance. "Better leave that broom right where it is and go find out what he's hollerin' about."

"Or I can leave out the back door and you can tell him I had an emergency." I shoot her a wide grin.

"Right." Donna huffs out a laugh. "One of us actually needs to keep this job."

"You've been working for him for twenty years. I think if anyone's job is in jeopardy, it's mine." I try pouting my lip, but Donna simply smiles.

I grab the broom, take a deep breath, and head in the direction of my father's office. It's slightly open when I reach it, and he's going over paperwork on his desk. I keep my eyes on the gold plaque on his desk that reads *Dr. Henry Canó* just for a second before I make myself look at him.

"You called?"

"You dropped Finite Math?" He raises his brown eyes to mine. "Why on earth would you do that? Do you want to stay in school forever? Is that it?"

"No." I bite my lip, looking down at the floor.

"You're already on thin ice. You do know that, right?"

I nod, staying quiet, mostly because the knot in my throat won't let me get words out, and also because I've learned that when speaking to my parents sometimes the best thing to do is not speak at all. My silence is what they want anyway. That way they can have the satisfaction of ridding themselves of all of their accusations.

"What class did you pick up?"

"None yet," I mumble.

"I cannot hear you or see your eyes," Dad snaps.

"None yet." I raise my eyes to his and straighten my posture. "I was going to take college algebra, but the class is full."

"Why'd you drop this one?" he asks again. This time, I don't even bother with excuses, even if any excuse I come up with would certainly be more credible than the reality.

"There's a boy in the class that I would rather avoid." I bite my lip as my father's eyes turn from fury to incredible as he stares at me. I do my best not to flinch as I wait for the onslaught of words, but they never come.

"Come here." He sighs deeply and shakes his head. I walk

over to his desk tentatively, dragging the broom behind me. He turns his chair toward me. "Is it Lawrence?"

"No." My face pulls. "Lawrence and I are over and he goes to Duke, remember?"

Even as I say this, dad's face pinches into a disgusted look. My parents are hardcore UNC alumni, so when I met and started dating Lawrence, Duke's star quarterback, they both had a lot to say, all in good fun, of course, though times like these, when dad lets his feelings on the matter show, are more telling than any joke he'd ever make.

"So this is just some random boy?" Dad asks with a laugh. "You were with Lawrence for what, two and a half years?"

"Yes." I swallow. Closer to three, but I'd rather not go there. "And yes, we still hate him."

"We absolutely do." Dad smiles. "If he'd been in that classroom, would you have dropped it?"

"No." I scowl. "Eff that guy."

Dad chuckles. "You see where I'm going with this, right?"

"Yeah."

"Is this boy bullying you?"

"No." I scoff. "Come on, Dad."

"So what are you afraid of?"

"I'm not afraid." My scowl deepens. "I would just rather avoid him is all."

"Listen," Dad starts with an exhale. "I am not going to tell you I understand this situation because you're giving me very little to go on, but this boy isn't worth you having to stay in college an extra semester. You have to see that."

"I do."

"Get back in that class." He taps his mouse and the school website appears on the screen. I close my eyes momentarily and log into my account, picking up Finite Math once more.

"For the record, I hate math," I grumble.

"Trust me, the last three years have proven math hates you more than you hate it." He glances over at me, amusement in his expression.

"Funny, Dad." I exit out of my account and take a step back as Dad laughs. "Does this mean I can stop cleaning the practice after hours?"

"Do you think you've earned enough hours to pay for the Maserati you crashed?"

"No." My shoulders slump.

"Are you still dead set on moving into that house instead of just moving back in with me and Mom?"

"No offense, Dad, but I hope I never have to live with you and Mom ever again." I smile at the look on his face. "Besides, I don't want to drive forty minutes to and from school."

"Right."

"Do you need any help filing those papers?" I nod toward his desk.

"Nah. Let Donna do the filing. I have to be in the OR at seven in the morning, so I'm going over the procedure one last time." He stands up and walks over to me. "See you Sunday?"

"Fine." I give him a quick hug and walk to the door.

"Adrian says you picked up shifts at the bar."

"Yeah." I idle by the door. "I used the money you gave me

for the deposit, but that'll only cover a month, so I told Uncle Adrian I'd help out at the bar a few days a week."

"As long as it doesn't compromise your GPA." Dad raises an eyebrow.

"It won't."

"Good." He gives one final nod before I leave his office.

It takes me a good hour before I actually leave the practice behind and head to my uncle's bar on the other side of town. When I get there, I park in the employee parking in the back, walk in through the back door, which is always unlocked, and head to the kitchen.

"Josephine Canó," Donovan, the head chef says. "I heard you were going to start working here but I could not believe it."

"Don't worry, I'm not coming for your job."

"You bet your ass you're not, unless you're going to attend the best culinary school in the country and go train in France." He raises an eyebrow.

"Yeah, no. I can barely cook chicken." I smile. "I'll be manning the bar."

"The bar." Donovan gives me an appreciative nod. "Where the tips are."

"Exactly." I laugh.

"I heard about that little accident you got into. What were you thinking?"

"I wasn't. That's the problem."

"You totaled it then? A freaking Maserati?"

"That's what they're accusing me of."

"What you driving now? Your daddy give you your old car back?"

"Hardly." I scoff. "But a car is a car, right?"

"What kind of car is it?" The gleam in his eyes tells me he probably already knows, but I play along anyway because Donovan is like an uncle to me and all my uncles are full of jokes and leg pulling.

"Celica. It's like a ninety-two or something with a non-existing heater and a messed-up radio."

"Daaaaaamn." He laughs loudly. "The fall from grace was bad, huh?" He laughs again. "What color is it?"

"Gold." I scowl, but I'm trying really hard not to laugh along with him even though he's being a total asshole.

"Gold." He laughs louder. "Shit. My brother had that car in high school." He stops laughing. "Did your dad buy it from him?"

I shrug. "Probably. Who else has junk cars lying around?"

"Damn, Jo. Have you ever even driven a used car?"

"I have now."

"I want to feel sorry for you, but I always did say you and your sister were too spoiled for your own good." He shakes his head.

"I know." I sigh. "We are."

"I bet Misty is being extra careful with her Benz these days."

I nod, hoping my expression tells him I want this conversation to be over already. Of course, Donovan knows I didn't want to have this conversation to begin with, but here we are.

"See you later, Don." I start walking toward the door that leads to the bar.

"Later, Jojo."

"I thought I saw that junk car of yours in the cameras," Uncle Adrian says with a wide smile when I reach the bar.

"Hilarious. You're all a bunch of grade A comedians here," I deadpan.

"Aw, come on, Jo. We're just messing with you." He pulls me into a quick hug. "You ready to work?"

"Work? I came here to drink. I told you I'd start in two days."

"Yeah, well, Marissa called out and it's college night, so I kinda need extra hands."

"Okay." I take a deep breath.

How bad can it be to serve a bunch of college kids half-priced drinks and ninety-nine cent beers?

Chapter Two

Jo

I T'S BAD.

They're rowdy and demanding and keeping up with the orders is proving to be a pain in the ass. There's a loud slap of hands on the bar in front of me and I glance up to see a guy on the other side. I have to do a double take and in my overwhelmed state it takes me a full minute to realize who he is, and when it hits me, I stop wiping the glass in my now shaky hands and look up at him again. He's tall, with a natural golden tan, defined muscles, a chiseled jaw, voluminous dark hair, and unforgettable piercing toffee-colored eyes. Memories flood me quickly, and I chase them away twice as fast.

"We asked for a round of tequila shots well over ten minutes ago," he says, his deep voice hitting me right in the chest.

"I'll be right over," I say, glancing around for Patrick, who's probably the one working their table. "We're extremely under-staffed today."

"I've seen Marissa man this bar by herself, so I wouldn't say having two people working is being understaffed." He raises an eyebrow.

I grip the side of the bar and lean in so that I don't have to yell over the loud music. "I know it's difficult for a hot shot, spoiled brat like you to sit and wait for a couple of minutes while other patrons who were actually here before you are served, but I'm not Marissa and I'm not going to drop everything I'm doing and fall all over myself just so you and your brothers can get a shot of tequila." My eyes narrow on his. "Wait your turn."

"This is bullshit," he grits out.

"Take it up with management."

"Right, because management is going to do something about it when you're their little fucking princess." He scoffs.

"Go back to your table, Jagger. I'll have someone out there with your shots momentarily." I stare at him.

He stares back with just as much annoyance in his eyes before turning around and stomping back over to his table. I take nice long breaths to calm down and go right back to what I was doing. When I look down, I laugh. His ticket was next. If he'd just waited at his table, he would have drunk his stupid shot by now. The ticket doesn't specify what kind of tequila he wants, so I serve him our most expensive one and take out a tray of six glasses to his table. The Cruz brothers are gorgeous, drop-dead gorgeous, if you're into hyperboles, except their gorgeousness isn't an exaggeration.

They truly are the epitome of sexy, with their tanned complexions that has nothing to do with self-tanners or the sun, and everything to do with their dark-skinned father, who happens to be my father's good friend. One of them got green eyes from his mother, while the other two have brown eyes, but only Jagger's smoldering toffee-colored eyes can make anyone's heart flip. Or maybe it's just that Maverick, the youngest, hasn't figured out what to do with all that swagger he was blessed with. Despite our parents being friends and us seeing one another a lot growing up, I haven't seen them in years, with them living in New York and all. I set the tray down on the table, doing my best to ignore Jagger's glare, because I don't have to look at him to know he's definitely glaring. He always is. At me, anyway. He's perfectly cordial and charming to everyone else.

"Hey! I didn't know you worked here, Jo," Maverick says, picking up two shot glasses. "I haven't seen you in a minute."

"First day here." I smile. "You've grown up."

"I have." He grins and it hits me just how grown up he is.

"Hey, Jo," Mitchell says, smiling at me. "Is Misty working here too?"

"Nope."

"I heard about the car accident. I'm glad you're okay," Mav adds.

"Thanks." I give him a tight smile. Leave it to my mother to gossip about her own daughter's car accident, no doubt she told Mildred Cruz *everything*.

"I haven't seen you in a while," Mav says. "How long has it been? A year? Two?"

"A long time."

"Where you been? You still dating the quarterback for Duke?" Mitch asks, his mouth pulling with disgust.

"Lawrence," Mav supplies.

"Oh shit. Right." Mitch glances over at Jagger momentarily.

"Nope. We're done."

"How's your sister?" Mitch asks.

"She's doing really well." I smile. "I'll tell her you say hi."

"Please do." He smiles.

Misty had been heartbroken for nearly a year when Mitch broke off their summer fling and told her he didn't do long distance. I didn't understand her hang up since they weren't even together that long, but then I did the stupidest thing when I ran into Jagger freshman year and hooked up with him. A stupid, drunken, rookie mistake and I fully grasped why she'd been so heartbroken. I only had one night with Jagger and felt like I could have easily spiraled down the rabbit hole he would've no doubt led me to. My sister spent three months with Mitch. If they were anything alike, providing their undivided attention to a woman and making them feel special, I knew a breakup had to be awful. There aren't many things I regret, but that one-night stand was something I could say for certain I'll regret for the rest of my life. Ever since then, I've done everything in my power to stay away from him and vowed to take that little secret rendezvous to the grave. Not even Misty knows about that and my sister is my best friend.

"I would ask if you're going to the barbecue on Sunday but I heard you always skip those," Mav says.

"Hm. I usually do, but I might just go this time." I usually skip the barbecues my parents throw because they coincide with the one Lawrence used to take me to for his own college, but now that we're done, I might as well drop by for this one.

"I'll have another shot." Jagger sets down both shot glasses in front of him with a clink. "Two more rounds for all of us. Maybe you'll bring them in the next hour this time."

"It was good to catch up." I smile at Mav and Mitch as I grab all six glasses and put them on my tray and walk away, seething.

It's one thing for him to berate me privately, but in front of his brothers? Fuck him.

Chapter Three

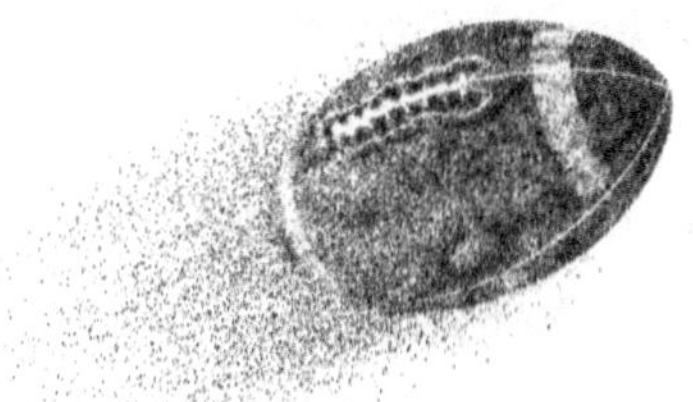

$\mathcal{J}o$

RUSH OVER TO THE DOOR AND PULL IT OPEN. I MADE SURE TO GET here fifteen minutes early so that I can pick where I want to sit—all the way in the back row of the classroom. It's a big one, too. Finite Math isn't normally for upperclassmen, certainly not for seniors like me, but Mom said it was the easiest math course and I just really needed to pass, so here I am. I'm a straight A student in everything else. My parents have never understood how a girl who has had math tutors her entire life just can't get a handle on the subject, and honestly, I don't understand it either. I slide into the furthest chair from the professor's desk, which also happens to be the furthest chair from the side door. I'm about to move closer to it when it opens and a slew of students step inside. Keeping my head down, I take out a pen and notebook. On the syllabus, there are clear instructions about having no computers in class.

The professor walks in and smiles, saying hello to the class before taking a seat behind the desk and opening her bag. She starts taking out papers and stacking them on her desk. She seems nice. According to Mom, who works here as well and gets the dirt on everyone, the professor recently came back from maternity leave, which makes sense. She's absolutely glowing. The side door opens again and I don't look, but instantly know who just walked in, judging by the chatter that started. I slide lower in my seat, hoping to avoid him at all costs. When I went down the list of names of the people in the class and saw his, I instantly dropped it, but after picking it back up, I told myself he'd probably never show up anyway. After all, he's also a senior, he's a jock, and he shouldn't need to sit in for this.

Heavy footsteps ring out beside me, and even though I'm trying to do everything in my power not to look up, I find that I can't ignore him. I glance up and meet his eyes, instantly regretting it.

"You're in my seat."

"There are no assigned seats." I blink, shooting him the dirtiest look I can muster. He seems to find this amusing, his eyes gleaming as he stares at me.

"All right." He shrugs a shoulder and sits in the chair beside me. A chair that's ridiculously close to mine. I set the tip of my sneaker on the side of it and he meets my gaze again. "What are you doing?"

"Trying to push you away."

"Wouldn't you say you succeeded in pushing me away?" He raises an eyebrow, eyes boring into mine. Heat pricks my skin.

"I mean . . . you don't have to sit so close to me."

"You're in my seat. This is the next best thing."

"There's only been one class so far. How is this your seat?"

"Because I always sit in the back left of the class. You'd know that if you paid attention to your surroundings more often."

"What's that supposed to mean?" I frown. "I've never had a class with you."

"Never?"

"Not since freshman year." I swallow.

"And you dropped it, didn't you?" He tilts his head slightly, examining my expression.

"I don't see why that's any of your business." I lower my foot, straighten in my chair, and look at the front of the room.

"Why are you in this class, anyway?"

"Because I have no choice. Why are you here?"

"Same reason. Your mom told me this is the easiest A, so here I am."

"Hm." I scowl. My mother is a traitor.

"You still studying, what was it, nursing?"

"Public health."

"Public health?" His brows raise. "What are you going to do with that?"

"I can do different things, but I'm looking into becoming a PA."

"PA?" Jagger nods slowly. "I would've bet money on your becoming a doctor."

"Because of my dad?"

"Yeah, I guess." He chuckles, stretching his legs. I inhale

sharply, moving mine quickly so his don't touch mine. "I'm still political science. Thinking about law school."

"Law school?" I raise my eyebrows. "Don't you have like every scout in the country looking at you?"

"Yeah." His lips flatten and I can tell I hit a sore subject, though I can't imagine why. He's destined to play in the NFL. At least, that's what I've always assumed.

"Hm," is the only comment I make.

"You still playing volleyball?"

"Nope." I cross my arms. Now it's my turn to avoid the subject.

"Hm," he says back and doesn't comment further, just that grunt of acknowledgement, and I focus on class, rather than him and his long legs, giant frame, and obnoxiously sexy voice.

I pick up my pace as I near the house and furthermore when I see people walking on the sidewalk. I knew this house was coveted, but I didn't realize by how many until I got the alert that I was next in line for it on a list of 80. It's a cute little cottage, the kind people dream of settling down in, with an evergreen exterior and white picket fence surrounding it. Settling down is a far cry from what happens here though, and everyone knows it. In the past, it's been housed by fraternities and sororities alike. Now that Greek life has its own row of houses a block away from here, it's housed by upperclassmen and women. People like me, who are tired of small beds and noisy hallways and want to live off campus. People like me, with connections to owners of houses like this one. Or rather, my parents are the ones with the connections and I'm the one who reaps the benefits of that. I take the steps two at a time, ignoring everyone in my wake and surroundings.

If I know one thing is not to make eye contact with people you're passing—in line, in life. It's the reason I stay to myself mostly. It's the reason I never joined a sorority, like my best friends did. I do reap the benefits of those connections as well though, and go to the important parties here and there. At least I did, before Lawrence told me it made him jealous and I stopped altogether. *Jealous my ass.* My throat burns as I think about my cheating ex-boyfriend Lawrence and my ex-friend Crystal. I force myself to shove the emotion away before I start crying. As it is, I'm overdue for a good cry. I've been holding all of these emotions in, waiting for the right moment to let them loose, but I've been too busy to have a legitimate emotional breakdown.

I reach for the door just as someone else places their hand over mine. The touch makes me jolt and bounce back. I glance up quickly, meeting toffee eyes. His gaze burns into mine, his lips forming a hard line. I swallow, shaking my head because there's no way, *there's no way*, except it would be just my luck.

"What are—" My question is cut off by the door opening beside us. Neither of us look away from each other, unable to break this godforsaken spell that seems to always take hold when we're near each other.

"Miss Canó? Did I say that correctly?"

"Yes, ma'am." I blink away first, looking at the woman holding the door open.

"Mr. Cruz?"

"Yes, ma'am."

My pulse quickens. That voice, Jesus Christ, so deep and rich and punchable.

"Come in, please." She steps aside and I walk inside first. "I'm Lauren. My siblings and I own this house, but I'm the closest, so I'll be the one dropping in to check on it occasionally. We didn't used to do this, but after the incident, well, let's just say not checking in would be catastrophic."

"What incident?" I ask, frowning as we walk past the small living room with the fireplace and toward the kitchen.

Lauren's version of a tour, apparently, is walking swiftly past the rooms. We stop at the threshold of the kitchen. It's small, but has definitely been remodeled, with stainless-steel appliances.

"The fire," Jagger says, again, making my pulse quicken and heart drop into my stomach.

"I didn't hear about a fire."

"You must have been busy, probably with your asshole boyfriend." He says the words so casually, Lauren laughs. They continue walking and I stand there, stunned for a second, before picking up my pace and following behind them. The mere mention of my asshole boyfriend makes my insides burn, but the last thing I want is to tell Jagger he was right about Lawrence.

"The last tenants started a fire somehow," Lauren explains. "Anyway, the entire house was remodeled because of it, which explains the hike in rent, but both of you already paid for the semester, so that shouldn't be a problem."

"Wait." I blink, looking at Jagger. "Both of us . . . meaning . . . you're moving in here?"

"It appears so."

"Here?" I point at the floor beside me. "To this house?"

"Yep."

"I can't . . . " I shake my head slowly. When I clicked the box saying I was okay with living with a guy I was not expecting *him* to be the guy. "We can't . . . "

"I agree." Jagger cocks his head, crossing his arms. "You should take your deposit back."

"Me?" I press my hand to my chest. "You take your deposit back."

"And forfeit the place to you? To *Lawrence?*"

"What does Lawrence have to do with anything?"

"You tell me." He raises an eyebrow.

My face heats instantly at the memory he elicits with three little words. They were the words he'd said to me when I told him I was dating someone and could never, ever hook up with him again. It was that same night he told me Lawrence was a serial cheater. My stomach tightens. I shake my head. There's no way I can live with him. I'd agreed to be roommates with whomever they paired me with, thinking that I could get along with anyone, but this was clearly impossible. Jagger hates me and I return those feelings to be sure. And really, universe? I mean, I've managed to stay away from the guy for years and now this? There's no freaking way.

"Is there a problem?" Lauren asks.

"Do you have any other properties available?" I look at her because I definitely can't look at him right now.

"Classes already started." She raises an eyebrow. "This is it." She looked at the two of us. "Unless you want to try the dorms . . ."

"No." We both say it with finality in unison.

"I haven't lived in the dorms since freshman year," Jagger says. "Maybe you want to try the dorms again for your fourth year in a row?"

"I guess someone's been keeping score on my life," I shoot back.

"So, will you make it work or should I look for someone else?" Lauren looks between the two of us. "I have other people outside waiting just in case."

"We'll make it work." I take the keys she's holding out from her hand and follow her to the door.

"I'll email the final contract to each of you." She smiles. "Enjoy, and please don't burn the place down."

"We won't." I smile as she closes the door behind her, then exhale as I turn to Jagger, who is standing just a few feet away, watching me.

"You're really going to stay here?" he asks.

"Where else would I go? You heard her."

"I assumed your daddy could get you out of this somehow." He scowls. "Or your boyfriend."

"Not that it's any of your business, but I'm trying not to count on my father for anything." I lick my lips and look away.

"And I'm sure you heard me when I told your brothers that I'm no longer dating Lawrence."

"Right, right. You finally saw the light."

"What is your problem?" I meet his eyes again. "Seriously, what is your problem? You've been nothing but rude every single time I've seen you, which is a lot these last few days."

"I agree." He starts walking toward me.

My heart jumps with each step he takes. By the time he stops directly in front of me, I feel like I'm shaking. He reaches a hand out and my mouth falls open—to ask, to plead, to talk— but I can't form any words, and when his fingers graze mine and he leans into me ever so slightly, I think I'm a goner. The tip of his mouth pulls up as he grabs something out of my hand and pulls away. He brings his hand up and dangles a key, his key, I realize.

"I guess you're about to start seeing a lot more of me. See you later, *Roomie.*" He winks and turns away, leaving me standing there balking like an idiot.

Better that than the alternative. Better that than him kissing me, right? I'm not sure. I never was and never will be, but it's fine because it's not going to happen again. Especially now. Definitely not now. I have to keep my wits about me if I want to survive living in the same house as Jagger Cruz.

Chapter Four

Jagger

"YOU DID NOT JUST SAY WHAT I THINK YOU SAID." MAVERICK doubles over in laughter. "Hold up."

"Stop." I kick his ankle lightly. "People are staring."

"People are always staring at us."

"You gonna work out or what?" Mitch yanks his earphones off his head, the Kendrick Lamar song he's listening to blasting loudly now as he sets the bar down and sits up on the bench.

"I'm just here for moral support. My shoulder's still healing," I say.

Unfortunately, I'm nursing an injury that took me from being starting tight end to sitting out the last few games of the season last year. It took all summer for me to accept that I may be done with football. All summer of watching my father's old major league baseball videos and sorting through photos with the family. Since he's officially being inducted into the Baseball

Hall of Fame, we were asked to pick out some family pictures and old videos of him, all while I sulked and tried to mend my shoulder back to health, knowing that it might not be enough. Throughout it, my parents gave me lectures about how life is more than just about one thing. My father, who lived and breathed baseball, and my mother who lived and breathed track until she hung up her cleats after she got pregnant with Mitch, but that was after she'd won a gold Olympic medal. What they really wanted to do was berate me for giving up baseball and becoming a football player instead, but they didn't. That part was said in silence.

To say my summer was difficult is an understatement, but I'm fine now. At least I thought I was, until my brothers and I came back to North Carolina and I started working out with them again. Mav is a freshman and on the UNC hockey team. Mitchell is a junior and plays baseball. He was, to everyone's surprise, the only one who followed in our father's footsteps. Everyone expected us to play baseball because it's what you're expected to play if you're Dominican. We just happened to be athletic as hell and were good at most sports. Growing up, we dabbled in hockey, baseball, and football and could have secured a scholarship in either of the three sports, but football was what really captured me in high school.

Part of me always thought I turned my back on baseball because I knew it was so important to my dad. Too important. And his legacy was not something I could bear on my shoulders. A small part of me always wonders what if though, especially when I go to Mitch's games. Especially when I go to those games with Dad and see the pride in his face. No one would bat an eye if I decided to switch sports, but football was what made my adrenaline spike and I loved that feeling. My brothers and I were always at the top in our respective sports. The best in our high school, the top ten in our state, top thirty in the country. So, yeah, hurting my shoulder absolutely crushed me, because even if I don't make it as a starter in the NFL, I could have definitely made a team as a backup. I'm sure of it. Maybe I still can. I'm just not sure I'm willing to open myself up to the failure if I don't.

"Jag, why don't you tell Mitchell how you're rooming with Josephine Canó," Maverick says, pulling me away from my thoughts.

"No shit." Mitch starts laughing. "In that cute little cottage by campus? You and Jo? Surrounded by a white picket fence?"

"Fuck you both." I groan, running a hand through my hair. I'm not thrilled about rooming with Jo, but at least this conversation is a welcome distraction. "What the hell am I supposed to do?"

"You can just give back the deposit and move back in with me," Mav suggests. "Blanca and I are over for good."

"You say that every time Blanca and you break up." I shoot him a look.

"This time it's real. She's moving back to California to pursue the filmmaking thing and, well, you know how I feel about long distance."

"Speaking of long distance," Mitch says. "Does that mean Misty's moving in too?"

"No." I scowl. "What the hell would I know? I can't even wrap my head around seeing Jo three times in a week after not seeing her for over a year."

"That's because she was living closer to Duke before."

Closer to Duke. I feel my jaw twitch. Closer to Lawrence. Lawrence, who's still the star quarterback for the Blue Devils. Fuck that guy.

"I ran into Dr. Elsa," Mav says before I get a chance to ask how he knows that.

"When?"

"When I went to speak to my academic advisor." He looks at me with a raised brow. "I asked about Misty and Jo and she filled me in. They've been going through some shit after their grandfather died."

"Right." I look away. My brothers attended the funeral. I chose to stay in New York drowning my sorrows over my shoulder in a bottle of Macallan and random pussy.

"Look, you can either stay mad because she chose Lawrence over you or you can let it go and start over. Either way, you're not going to be able to avoid each other anymore."

"We'll see." My lips purse.

Every time Lawrence is mentioned, the sour taste in my mouth returns. It's not just that she picked him over me, it's that Lawrence and I have been in competition most of our lives, and even though it was friendly before, it felt personal when he made the moves on Josephine. The fact that she let him, that she fell for his southern charm, is what really kills me. Not that I'd ever admit that to her.

Chapter Five

Jo

"**I** THINK THAT'S IT, RIGHT?" MISTY ASKS. "YOU DON'T HAVE much. I'm kind of surprised."

"The place is furnished. Besides, I dropped the rest of my stuff back at Mom and Dad's."

"Did you pick your room?" She sets down the bags in the living room and shuts the door as I set the bags in my hands down as well.

"Not yet."

"I already picked." Jagger's voice booms from the hallway.

He runs a hand through his thick hair as he walks over to us, wearing a baby blue UNC Athletics T-shirt and basketball shorts. I try not to give him the pleasure of catching me checking him out.

"Hey, Jag," Misty says beside me. "I heard you got lucky and were paired to live with my favorite sister."

"Your only sister," I add.

"You mean she got lucky." He raises an eyebrow and walks over to Misty pulling her into a quick hug. "You moved back? I thought you decided to take a year off to travel?"

"Have you met my dad?" She shoots him a look that makes him laugh. "That was short-lived. I only took one semester off before starting. I've been at Duke for a while now."

"Duke?" Jagger groans. "Why?"

Misty laughs. "I guess it was my way of getting back at my parents. Like, yeah, I'll go to school, but it's going to be the one you don't approve of as much."

"Gutsy." Jagger grins. "So what are you studying? Something in the medical field?"

"Journalism, actually." She laughs. "I know. I know. Everyone thought I'd be a nurse or something."

"Journalism? Nice. I bet my mom would be glad to offer you a job at the magazine."

"I've thought about interning there, actually. I'll have to see how next summer looks." She moves closer and nudges me. "Jo's the one with the perfect GPA. Dad wants her to go to med school instead of PA school."

"She always was a huge nerd." Jagger's eyes dance as he looks over at me.

"Yeah, okay." I roll my eyes. "I'm going to go pick my room."

"I already told you, I picked for you."

"That's not how this works. You see why this is impossible?" I look at my sister and move past Jagger and make my way down the hall. "As it is, we have to share a freaking bathroom."

"We shared a tub when we were kids," he says, his voice close behind me. "Remember?"

"Unfortunately." I shut my eyes.

This is a mistake. I just broke up with my boyfriend, which means I definitely should not be feeling this way when another man speaks to me, but here I am, heart pounding in my throat, hands sweaty.

"I picked this room for you, by the way." His voice is still too near, too deep, too seductive, and I know him, he's not even trying to get to me, this is him without turning up the charm at all.

I take a deep breath and look around the room. It's nice enough. Queen-size bed, television, closet, dresser. I turn around and nearly slam right into his chest, which is exactly at eye level with me since I'm wearing flats and he's a giant. I crane my neck to meet his eyes.

"Excuse me. I want to see your room."

"Go right ahead." He moves out of the way and follows me to the room across the hall.

Like, right across the hall. Literally two steps away since the hall is so narrow. I let out a laugh as I push the door open. It's the same exact layout as the other room, but this bed is bigger and takes up a lot more of the room. He has three open bags, two on the floor and one on the bed, and clothes everywhere already, which makes me wonder how much time he beat me back here by.

"So, you get the king size?" I shoot him a look over my shoulder.

"I'm bigger than you. I thought it was only fair."

"Right." I sigh, walking out of the room. "I'm only letting you keep it because I'm not in the mood to argue right now."

"Josephine Canó doesn't want to argue?"

"I really don't." I walk back to the living room, where Misty is typing away on her phone.

"I know I said I'd help you unpack, but I have to get back. My landlord is at my new place." She looks up at me with a sigh.

"It's okay. I'm okay." I offer her a smile, but whatever she sees on my face makes her expression turn sad and sympathetic. She steps forward and wraps her arms around me, squeezing me tight.

"I'm so sorry I have to leave you like this. Just focus on unpacking, or don't. Take a nap. Go for a jog. Come out to the party tonight. It's a block away, so you can walk there and back." She pulls away and wipes the tears from my face. "You're stronger than you know."

"I just . . . " I nod, swallowing the lump in my throat. "I hate him."

"I know." She hugs me again and sighs. "I'm serious about the jog. It's a nice day out and it'll help clear your head."

I nod, wiping my tears as I pull away. I decide to do as she says and unpack and go for a jog afterwards. Jagger's in his room, door closed, playing music, so it's not like he's going to notice what I'm doing. I'm grateful for the space he's put between us, and even more grateful when I hear him leave the house right before I go for a jog. My sister's right, it helps clear my head and stop thinking about Lawrence every five seconds.

Chapter Six

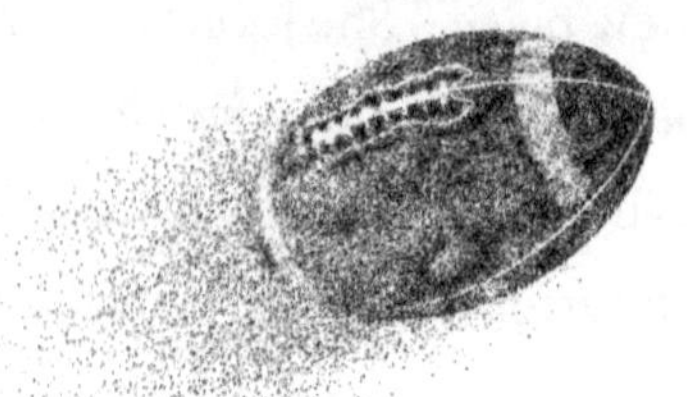

Jagger

"**W**HAT ARE YOU SO RILED UP ABOUT?" MAVERICK ASKS AS I walk over.

"Who says I'm riled up? I'm fine." I grab one of the red cups from his hand and take a sip, my mouth souring as the liquid goes down my throat. "God. This tastes like poison."

"It's the punch the sorority is known for." Mav glances at me. "How would you know what poison tastes like?"

"Well, if there was ever something poison would taste like it's this."

"I hear it sneaks up on you and knocks you on your ass."

"This stuff?" I chuckle, taking another sip. "Yeah right."

"Famous last words." He raises an eyebrow and takes another sip, cringing. "You're right though. Is it me or is it really sour?"

"It's kind of sour." I take another sip for good measure.

"Jagger!" The voice is shrilled in my ear as someone attempts to jump on my back.

I turn sideways and see Jessa with a wide smile on her face. She's wearing shorts that I know will give everyone a view of her nice ass and a shirt so small that all you can see is her cleavage, or the cleavage she managed to make with what she's working with. I fucked her last year, on and off, so I know exactly what she's working with.

"Hey, Jessa." I smile at her. "Who are you here with?"

"My sisters." She points at the four girls behind her, who are ogling me and my brother, and states their names as the goes.

"Nice to meet you, ladies." I nod.

"You've met them before." Jessa rolls her eyes and looks over at her friends. "He forgets everyone."

"I do. I'm sorry." I shoot them a sympathetic smile. "Do any of you have anything to do with the poison we're drinking?"

"It's so good, right?" Jessa puts a hand on my forearm and squeezes. "I would give you the recipe but then I'd have to kill you."

"I'd love to see you try." I raise an eyebrow and take another sip. Two of her friends have already taken a place on either side of Mav and are talking to him.

"Maybe I'll show you." She lowers her eyes and her voice as she steps even closer to me, smashing her tits on my arm. "I wouldn't object if you take me home tonight."

"Maybe I will." I meet her bright blue eyes and wink. She smiles wider.

"I have to introduce my Littles to some people, but I will be back to cash in on that offer." She leans in closer, pulling me down slightly until her mouth is near my ear and swirls her tongue along the shell. My cock stirs. She lets go and pulls away. "See you later."

"See ya." I put my cup up as a goodbye and watch the five of them walk away.

"She's fucking hot," Mav says beside me.

"She is."

"I don't understand why you don't just lock it down."

"Lock it down?" I turn to look at him.

"Make her your girlfriend, you know."

"Why would I?"

"Because she's fucking hot."

"And?" I raise an eyebrow. "Why don't you have a girlfriend?"

"Why would I? I just got here, I'm on the hockey team, I'm hot, you want me to keep going?"

"So I'm assuming you're saying I'm none of those things?" I laugh, shaking my head.

"I'm just saying, you already played the field and ran through all the hot girls here. You might as well settle down with one." He shrugs a shoulder. "Then again, what do I know, right?"

"I know you're going to learn this your way, but there's more to a relationship than being with a hot girl." I shoot him a look. "And there's more to being an athlete than just fucking all the hot girls."

"Says the guy who has spent the last three years fucking all the hot girls." Mav scoffs. "And still doesn't want a girlfriend."

I don't respond to that because what would I say? He's not wrong. I haven't really given the girlfriend thing much thought. I had a serious girlfriend in high school and we went our separate ways when she went to school in California and I chose UNC. As far as I know, she's in a serious relationship now and I'm happy for her. That doesn't mean I want to follow in her footsteps. Getting girls has always come easy for us. We're not too humble to disagree with that sentiment. We're also not so hung up on ourselves that we think anyone would be lucky to have us. Our parents raised us to believe in ourselves but to keep enough humility that we respect everyone. I'd like to say they did a fine job. It's one of the reasons I wouldn't officially date someone like Jessa. She's fun to fool around with but we have nothing in common outside of bed.

"When I meet the right girl, I'll settle down." I finish my drink and turn to him. "Want more poison?"

"Why not?" He shrugs a shoulder and follows me inside the house.

It's so crowded that if it weren't for our height, stance, and the fact that everyone knows us and parts slightly when we walk by, it would be impossible to walk in. We reach the kitchen, where the drinks are set up, and Mav pours new punch into our cups. I watch while he does it and suddenly feel like passing on the punch.

"You know anyone could have spit in our drinks, right?"

"They wouldn't."

"It's a punchbowl. They could throw anything in there." I examine the Kool-Aid-looking punch, unsure of whether or not I want to take the gamble on it now that I've seen where it comes from.

"Dude, you already had a drink."

"Yeah, that was before I saw this." My face pulls. "Did you pour it from here the first time?"

"Yeah." He stops pouring.

"And you didn't think maybe someone spit in it?"

"Of course I didn't think that. You'd have to be a freaking psycho to do that." He hands me the cup. "You want this or not?"

"Not. I'll just have a beer." I walk over to the cooler and grab a beer while Mav sips on the punch.

Soon, a huge guy walks into the kitchen with a smile on his face. "They told me you were here!"

"Luke." I give him a side hug when he gets close. "What's going on?"

"Not much. Missed you at practice the other day." He eyes me. "You gonna be okay?"

"I think so." I move my shoulder out of habit. "I'll be back Monday. Coach wants me to come in and learn the plays even if I don't go out on the field."

"Yeah, you should. Some of the guys are out back. You

wanna head over?" Luke nods toward the backyard. I look at my brother, who shrugs.

"Let's go."

I spend the majority of the night talking to my team-mates and hanging out with Mav. Mitch shows up when I'm almost leaving, and I end up staying longer than I wanted, and by the time I'm really ready to leave, Jessa shows up at my side and starts practically hanging from my arm.

Chapter Seven

Jo

"**I** DON'T THINK I WANT TO SMOKE THIS IN PUBLIC." I LIFT THE joint in my hand and look at Misty. "Can we go to your car?"

"So that it can reek of weed for the next century? No, thank you. If you wanted to hot box, you should've brought that nasty old Celica you're driving these days." Misty raises an eyebrow. "Besides, this is perfectly legal."

"Not here." I shoot her a look that makes her roll her eyes.

"It's not like you're going to get high out of your mind. Just high enough to relax. I mean, your doctor prescribed you Valium."

"For flying."

"It doesn't matter. Valium is a hardcore drug. This is all natural."

"I guess you're right." I press the joint to my mouth. "I just don't want someone to take a picture of me and post it somewhere. Dad would kill me."

"First of all, Dad won't care." Misty lights the joint and I inhale deeply and cough loudly as I exhale. "He literally was the one who got this for me from his doctor friend in Florida. Besides, who will take a picture of you? You're not that important."

I stick my tongue out at her. She doesn't mean it in a bad way. In all honesty, I'm not important in a *let's take a candid picture of her* sort of way. When I was dating Lawrence, I was. My heart squeezes. I cannot, will not, think about Lawrence right now. I can't have him ruining a night he's not even a part of. It's just hard since all the previous college parties I went to were with him and his friends and some of my volleyball teammates and now it's just me. And my sister.

"I think I'll stick to tequila." I hand over the little joint to her and grab my water bottle.

"Wow. Tequila." My sister laughs. "Your liver will hate you, but I guess that's a choice you have to make, right? Liver or lungs."

"That shouldn't even be a choice." I cap my water bottle and tuck it into my purse again.

"Well, we could do edibles."

"Last time you talked me into doing an edible I thought I was going to die, so I think I'll take my chances with my liver for now." I smile.

"In that case, I'll go get some shots," she says.

"Do these guys even have alcohol? This is a pretty tame frat party."

"It's a medical fraternity. They're into drugs, not alcohol," Misty says. "They're all probably doing drugs inside right now. You know, testing the limits of the brain and all that."

My eyes widen. I'm not a judgmental person, but that's a little off-putting.

She drops the joint into the small tube it came in and puts it in her bag and applies hand sanitizer before squirting some into my hands. "So, how's living with Jagger?"

"So far it's fine. It seems like we have opposite schedules. I haven't even seen him again." I walk beside Misty toward the house, taking in the guys stumbling out of it.

Maybe she's onto something and they really are all on drugs. I purse my lips, looking around the lawn as she pulls the door open. It really is a tame party, despite the stumbling guys. I'm used to seeing shirtless people running around the beer kegs.

"Has Lawrence reached out?"

"No." I swallow, my heart squeezing. "There's nothing to say. He's probably fucking Crystal."

"Jo." She reaches for my hand and squeezes. "I'm sorry you're going through it."

"Well, you went through it last year, so you get it." I shake my head. "Seriously, what is wrong with men?"

"Yeah, but I didn't catch Michael in the act and he took re-sponsibility and said it hadn't gone past flirting, so technically, he didn't cheat."

"Technically he was emotionally cheating. Some say it's worse."

"Is it?" She glanced up at me as she poured our shot glasses.

"No. I don't know. It's all hurtful."

"Exactly." She hands one over to me and clinks hers against mine. "To purging our lives of men."

"Here, here." I lift my glass and take a shot, my mind swimming instantly. When I open my eyes, I smile at her. "Let's do another."

After my third attempt to put the key in the lock, Misty takes them away from me and does it for me, ushering me inside.

"Careful with the step," I mumble.

"You're slurring," she says.

"So are you." I laugh. "Maybe weed isn't bad after all."

"I don't think the weed hit you. You're drunk." She pulls me toward the hall. "What room is it again?"

"That one." I point straight ahead.

"That's the bathroom."

Both rooms are shut, so I step forward and go left first. Might as well try both of them, right?

Misty grips my arm tighter, making me straighten. I pause and take a breath so I don't stumble. I took a pretty big fall on my way to the house. A funny fall. I mean, my knee hurts, but I laughed for an hour outside on the floor, so it obviously doesn't hurt that bad. Misty pushes the door open and gasps loudly, letting go of my arm and jerking away to rush down the hall.

"What are you doing?" I shout, then look inside the bedroom, where Jagger is lying naked with a naked woman on top of him.

I'm shocked into silence, staring at his muscular arms and large hands squeezing her waist. My entire body heats instantly and when her attention whips over to us, I feel sick.

"What the—" she says.

"What the fuck, Jo?" Jagger roars, raising his confused but livid gaze to us.

"Shit. Sorry." I shut the door quickly and stumble back. "I'm so sorry!"

I turn and run over to the living room, where Misty is picking up her purse.

"I called an Uber," she announces.

"You can't leave me right now," I whisper-shout.

"I can't stay!" Her mouth drops. "Come with me."

"I can't leave. This is my house too." I frown.

"So, you deal with it. I just saw Jagger Cruz fucking a woman and holy shit, Jo." Her eyes widen.

"We couldn't even see anything," I whisper.

"You're right, but what we saw is enough."

"I can't believe you're going to freaking leave me to deal with this." I point down the hall.

"Go to your room and go to sleep. It'll all be forgotten tomorrow," she says.

"Okay." I nod. That sounds completely possible. I kiss her cheek and lock the door behind her as she runs to her Uber.

As I undress, sloppily, because even in my drunken state I know I'm being sloppy, I think about what I saw. Jagger. A naked Jagger. Fucking a woman. Heat floods my entire body. I look at the door, wondering if they picked up where they left off, if they're still . . . I shiver. I shouldn't care. I don't care. Absolutely don't care. Yet, there's a twist of something deep in my stomach as I recall what I saw. Jealousy? There's no way. I mean, maybe there is a way. Maybe I'm jealous that someone is getting lucky while I'm just sitting here thinking about it in my underwear. There's commotion outside my room and I sit up straight. I can't hear what the voices are saying, but I do hear the door slam shut and the stomping in the hall just before the door opens suddenly.

"What are you—"

"You think this is funny?" Jagger asks. He's positively seething, shirtless, and seething, and holy shit he is so hot. So, so hot. I hate him, absolutely hate him, but damn. "You think it's funny to come home in this state and barge into my room in the middle of the night like that?"

I shake my head. I want to say I don't think it's funny at all, but I can't look away from his thunderous gaze and his chiseled jaw or his messy sex god hair and his ripped torso. Jesus. I knew Jagger was hot but this is beyond.

"I'm drunk," I say instead. "Like really drunk and I don't ever get drunk like ever and I am so mortified and so sorry. Truly."

His expression softens, not much, but enough. "We need to set up ground rules if we're going to make this living arrangement work."

"Okay."

"Good." He breaks his gaze from mine and lowers it to the rest of my body. His jaw twitches and I swear he looks more pissed off than he did a second ago.

"What?"

"Nothing." He swallows.

"Oh." I look down at myself and realize I'm wearing nothing but a strapless bra and ivory lace panties. "I . . . I was changing but then I couldn't find my pajamas and I mean, is it me or is it really hot in this house?"

"Yeah. Really hot." He lets out a laugh. "We'll talk in the morning." His jaw twitches again as he turns around and slams the door shut behind him, making me jump. He slams his own door shut as well, making me jump again.

Living with Jagger Cruz is definitely not for the faint of heart.

Chapter Eight

Jagger

"**I**'M SORRY ABOUT YESTERDAY." JO'S VOICE IS JUST ABOVE A WHISPER. "I never, ever get like that."

I shake my head. I'm not sure I've ever been able to hold a grudge against Jo and this is no different, but seeing her barge into my room while I was with Jessa was a lot to handle, especially since I'd been thinking of her. I told myself it was because she was my roommate now and she'd always been my what-if, but if I'm being honest with myself, I think about Jo a lot more often than I should. I shut my eyes and huff out a quiet laugh. It's pathetic, really, and something I'd never admit to anyone.

"Where'd you go last night?" I turn around with two mugs of coffee in hand and place them on the table in the kitchen.

"Frat party." She takes a sip of coffee. "Boring frat party."

"You went to a boring frat party and came home like that?" I raise an eyebrow.

"Yeah." She licks her lips. I look away. The last thing I need or want is to get caught up in those lips and wishing they were on mine. "I'd never smoked and then I started taking shots and . . . yeah. I guess I overdid it. I'm sorry I walked in on you like that. It wasn't on purpose."

"It was probably for the best." I take a sip of coffee. "But we do need to set up boundaries if we want this to work."

"I agree."

"No barging into each other's rooms without knocking," I say.

"That's fair." She presses her lips together. "You walked into my room without knocking too though."

"Because I knew you were alone."

"I could have been naked." She raises an eyebrow, but even as she does it, she blushes. I ignore the way her words and that blush seem to go straight to my cock.

"You practically were naked, Jo."

"I could have been touching myself." She glances away.

Her words throw me off, but as I stare at the side of her face, I decide that this conversation needs to be over because now I'm hard and there's no way in hell I'm ever going to try to hit on this girl again, not after what happened when we were freshmen. It's like I can't help myself though.

"Seeing me fucking someone makes you want to touch yourself?"

"No." Her face turns bright red as she meets my eyes. "I didn't even see anything. Not really anyway."

"But you would have liked to stay to watch?" I raise an eyebrow. "I can arrange that."

"Absolutely not." She scowls, dropping her gaze to the mug in front of her.

I enjoy my coffee in silence. I want her to be the one to set a rule or say something about her life, which I don't know much about anymore. I've made it a point to stay far away from Josephine Canó as long as she was with Lawrence, but she's no longer with him, so . . .

"No leaving clothes on the bathroom floor," she says after a moment.

"Okay."

"One of us goes grocery shopping every week. We split the cost of everything so we don't have to argue over who ate what."

"Has this happened to you?" I fight a smile. She looks upset about it and she always looks so damn cute when she's upset.

"My last roommate had a problem sharing everything from peanuts to apples."

"I thought you hated peanuts."

"You remember that?" She blinks up at me.

I want to tell her I remember everything about her, but don't, because it would make me sound like a loser and an idiot and I refuse to be either. I clear my throat. "So we split the grocery bill."

"Or we can go together."

"Where?"

"Grocery shopping."

"I don't go grocery shopping. I have it delivered."

"Of course you do." She rolls her eyes.

"What's that supposed to mean?"

"You always had everything done for you so I guess it should come as no surprise that you can't even buy your own groceries."

"I do buy my own groceries, from the comfort of my couch. And my mother didn't do everything for me."

"You're right. Your nanny did."

"Are we going to start arguing about the way we were brought up now, Jo?" I raise an eyebrow. "Because my nanny babysat you an awful lot."

"Yeah, when we were in New York and our parents left us at your house. Not all of us grew up like that though." She raises an eyebrow right now. "My parents are pretty well off and I've been doing my own laundry since I was twelve."

"Miss Responsible, huh?" I set my mug down. "Yet you managed to crash the most expensive car in your dad's lot."

"You heard about that, huh?" Her voice no longer holds the spunk it did a second ago and it makes me even more curious as to what happened that night. When I found out about the accident, I thought there was no way Jo was involved, but she was, and that made me even more upset because it made me realize I truly didn't know this person anymore.

"What were you doing driving that car? You can barely drive a golf cart."

"That is not true."

"Isn't it?" I chuckle. "As I recall, you crashed a perfectly good golf cart into a lake."

"I was thirteen!" She stares at me. "You seriously have the memory of an elephant and it's extremely annoying."

I chuckle. "In any event, you crashed the Maserati and now you're paying for it."

"Right. I'm definitely paying for it." She picks up her coffee. "I have to get to class, so if that's enough rules for you, then it's enough for me."

"What about parties?"

"What about them?" She stands up with her mug and heads to the hall.

"Are we allowed to have parties?"

"Do you want to have a party?" She turns to face me.

"Do you?"

"I mean . . . " She bites her lip for a second. "I know you guys love to throw parties, so I guess it's fine."

She means my brothers and me. Mitch and me specifically. Maverick just got here, so even though he's attended some of our parties, he hasn't had the pleasure of throwing one. It's something Mitch and I have been looking forward to—the three of us throwing a party together before Mitch decides whether or not he's going pro this year or next.

"We can throw like a housewarming party," Jo says after a moment.

"I guess." I chuckle. A housewarming party. Who is this girl?

"How many people?" She tugs her bottom lip into her mouth. I take a breath and focus on her eyes.

"I don't know. Do you want there to be a limit?"

"I don't want the place getting trashed or a fire to start and Lauren to sue us," she says. "When would this party take place?"

"Tonight?"

"I work tonight." She bites her lip. "But I'm totally okay with you having a party without me."

"It's our *housewarming*," I say, trying to fight a laugh. She looks at me, looks away, looks at me again. The fact that she's nervous definitely shouldn't be making me hard, right? Fuck I should have not kicked Jessa out last night. She didn't want to leave even after the interruption.

"Maybe next week?" she asks.

"Next week works. Friday?"

"Maybe?" She starts walking away, but idles by the threshold of the kitchen.

"Let's just play it by ear," I suggest. That seems to be the best solution for this right now.

"Perfect." That earns me a smile from her before she disappears down the hall.

I try my absolute hardest to not picture her naked the entire time the water is running in the shower, but I can't seem to stop the visual of walking into her room last night and her sitting there in nothing but her underwear. Fuck. How many times have I jerked off to her face and the idea of her body on mine? How many women have I fucked with the same visual? Too many. I take a deep breath and remind myself I can never go down that road again.

Chapter Nine

Jo

"How's that car treating you?" Donovan asks when I walk into the kitchen.

"It's so crazy." I walk over and stand across the counter he's currently working on, plating a meal. "It drove me all the way here."

"All the way here, you say?" He raises an eyebrow. "Who knew a car that doesn't cost six figures could do that."

"Funny, Donovan." I walk away as the rest of the kitchen staff laughs at his joke, and set my purse down in the break room, grabbing the black waist apron my uncle set in the cubby assigned to me and tying it around myself.

I wait until I walk out of the kitchen before picking up my hair into a high ponytail. I haven't straightened it in weeks, so the curls are bouncier and tighter than usual, but I do my best to smooth the top and bottom as I secure it. I take a breath before pushing the door that leads to the bar and smile when I see Marissa already there serving drinks. Marissa is a few years older than me but she's been working here since she was in high school, which feels like an eternity to me. I heard she tried to quit once and Uncle Adrian gave her a raise and offered to pay for her school. Obviously, she couldn't refuse that offer.

"Hey." She tucks her dark, straight hair behind her ears and glances over at me with a smile. "I was so happy to hear that you were joining us. Not happy about the reason, of course, but happy you're here."

"Thanks." I return her smile. "I think you're the first person to offer a bit of sympathy for what happened."

"I mean . . . " She tops off the beer she's pouring and turns to me. "I don't feel bad for you for working here, but it's gotta suck to crash that car."

"You have no idea." I sigh, then smile. "But I am glad to be here. It's long overdue."

"We'll split the first fifteen tables," she says, glancing up. I follow her gaze. "Patrick is handling the rest."

"Sounds good to me." I pick up the pad and pen in front of me and walk around the bar, heading to table one.

I'm wiping down table five when I see him walk in. My heart plummets. I gather the cloth and spray and bolt to the back of the bar.

"What's wrong?"

"My ex is here and I just can't." I must be showing my emotions in my expression, because Marissa shoots me a sympathetic look and looks toward the dining area.

"Tall, blond, Ken look-alike?"

"Yes." I shut my eyes, heart still hammering. If he's here with Crystal I will lose my shit. I just know it. And I can't afford to lose my shit.

"I'll take care of it," Marissa says. My eyes pop open. "I'll make sure Patrick serves him. It'll be fine."

"Thank you so much," I breathe. "I just can't do this right now."

"Hey, I get it." She looks toward the restaurant again. "We have new people at table five. You take care of those and Patrick will worry about your ex's table."

I take a second to compose myself, taking a deep breath and keeping my head high as I walk toward table five. Knowing Lawrence is here will not trip me up right now. He doesn't deserve to have that kind of power over me. I'm so focused on getting to table five that I don't actually see who's sitting there until I'm already in front of Jagger and his friend. That's when my heart starts working overtime. As I meet his eyes, it's impossible not to replay what I saw last night. Impossible to unsee his perfect abs or the veins in his arm as he flexed to grab the woman on top of him. That's the thought that puts a sour taste in my mouth and reminds me who I'm dealing with. Jagger Cruz. Womanizer. Player. Heartbreaker. My new roommate. The person I absolutely cannot see in that light. We were friends once, before we went and messed that up by hooking up. Maybe we can get back there. Maybe, but doubtful, because for some inexplicable reason, I feel things I shouldn't when I'm around him. Instead of looking at him, I focus on his friend, who's incredibly handsome, with silky, dark skin and long dreads that normally don't do it for me, but on this guy, they work.

"Hi." I smile. "My name's Jo and I'll be taking your order today. Have you had a chance to look at the menu?"

"How's the cacciatore?" the guy asks.

"Really good. I'm partial to the lasagna." I wink and lower my voice as if I'm letting him in on a secret, even though it's announced on the menu. "It's the owner's mother-in-law's recipe and it's legit."

"I'll have the lasagna then." He smiles, handing over the menu. I jot it down after plucking it from his hand and look at Jagger.

"I'll have the same." He hands me his menu.

"Do you want anything else to drink besides water?"

"Water is fine." Jagger picks up his glass and takes a long sip through his straw until it's obvious he needs a refill. So obnoxious. Such a Jagger thing to do. I resist the urge to roll my eyes or comment on it as I take it from the table when he sets it down.

"What do you have on tap? Anything local?" the friend asks.

"I can check for you." I glance at the bar briefly, but can't make out the labels on the handles from where I stand. "I'm new. Sorry."

"No worries. Take your time." His smile is warm as he gives me a once-over. I walk away and head back to the kitchen.

"Two lasagnas," I call out, tearing the paper from the pad and setting it on the queue for them.

I turn around and refill the glass with water before making my way back to their table, but before I can reach it, Lawrence walks up to me and blocks my path.

I freeze, meeting his clear blue eyes. "I'm working."

"We need to talk."

"We don't and even if we did, we can't talk while I'm working," I whisper-shout. "If you really wanted to talk, you would have called."

"Apologies shouldn't be said over the phone."

"I don't want another apology." I glare at him. "Leave it alone."

"I can't leave it alone." He lowers his voice and his head is closer to mine. My heart stops beating.

"If you kiss me I will throw this all over you and punch you and if I get fired you're going to have to pay me a lot of money."

"Fine. I'll wait." He steps back.

I swallow and continue moving, setting Jagger's water down on the table. I don't miss the pissed-off expression on his face before I turn away and move onto one of my other tables. There's something to be said about adrenaline and the way it pushes you out of your comfort zone because it propels me to move around the restaurant faster than I ever have.

I'm taking the trash out before leaving when Lawrence catches up to me again. I groan, wishing I'd let Patrick do it, like he said he would. That way, I would've already been safely in my car and driving away. Instead, I feel like I'm being emotionally attacked.

"Are you free now?" he asks, hands in his pockets.

I wish I could say I didn't miss him, but that would be a lie. After three years of feeling his arms around me, I can't really deny it, and it makes me feel even more insecure because why should I miss someone who hurt me the way he did? He cheated on me, who knows how many times, before I finally caught him with a person I thought was my friend.

"What do you want? Why are you even here?"

"I came to apologize."

"Now?" I shake my head. "How am I even supposed to take you seriously?"

"It took that long for me to realize how badly I'd fucked up."

"Yeah." I let out a laugh. "Okay."

"I'm sorry I hurt you." He walks forward. "Just . . . give me another chance. I'll make this right."

"What about Crystal?" I cross my arms.

"What about her? Who cares? That's old news." His eyes search mine. "It's over."

"Why'd you do it?" I hate the way my voice breaks.

"I don't know." He runs a hand through his blond waves. "I'm an idiot. I guess I let myself get caught up in the fact that I haven't been with anyone else since we got here and college is supposed to be this wild experience and . . . " He shrugs. "I'm the starting quarterback, babe. Do you know how many women throw themselves at me?"

"But you couldn't ignore my friend." My voice wavers. "I thought she was a friend."

"She was never your friend." His expression turns serious. "She was hitting on me the entire time you were friends."

My chest squeezes. "Is knowing that supposed to make me feel better?"

"No." He raises a hand and sets it on my shoulder. I pull away, putting distance between us. "I'm sorry. I just want to say I'm sorry and I want to try this again."

"No."

"Think about it. Are you going to the barbecue tomorrow?"

"Are you insane?" My voice is nearly a shriek.

The only reason I ever went to those Duke barbecues was because we were together, otherwise I wouldn't have been caught dead at a Duke function. As it is, my parents low-key judged me for choosing to go to those barbecues and not theirs since I'm a UNC student, they're UNC alumni, and my mother is a current employee, so you can say their hate for Duke goes deep in the already bad rivalry.

"Come on, Jo. Don't be like that."

"You cheated on me, Lawrence. You hurt me. I'm not giving you another shot. There's literally no way."

"None of this would have happened if you'd moved in with me."

"Now you're blaming me?" I laugh, even though I'm shaking. "That's rich."

"If you had moved in with me, she wouldn't have been able to entrap me the way she did."

"Entrap you." I shake my head and look away. "Wow."

"Just . . . let's put it behind us."

"I'm going to put it behind us but I'm not getting back together with you." I meet his eyes so he sees how serious I am. "There's no way in hell I'd ever date an athlete again. Ever."

He shakes his head, sighing heavily. "Just think about it. Please."

"Fuck you, Lawrence." I walk away quickly.

"Just think about it. Tell me you'll think about it." He catches my arm just as I'm reaching my car.

"Maybe you should have treated her right to begin with." Jagger's voice snaps our attention in that direction.

He's standing there with his friend beside him and they look menacing to say the least, Jagger with his jaw twitching and his body in a fighting stance and his friend, with the kind smile, is no longer smiling and is pretty freaking huge. It must be one of his teammates, which makes sense. The few times I've caught glimpses of Jagger through the years he's either been surrounded by women, his teammates, or his brothers.

"Why don't you mind your own fucking business?" Lawrence lets go of my arm. "This is between me and Josephine."

"And me now since I don't know how to mind my own

business." Jagger cocks his head, a lazy smile forming on his face. "Besides, my roommate's business is my business."

"Roommate?" Lawrence looks between Jagger and me before settling on me. "Is he serious?"

I swallow and nod. If I wanted to piss Lawrence off to begin with, I would have told him I was rooming with a guy. If I wanted to really piss him off, I would have said that guy was Jagger. I didn't bring it up because I'm not that petty and I just want this over. The last thing I need is to rehash frenemies and poke old wounds.

"Wow, Josephine." Lawrence barks out a laugh. "This is low even for you."

"Even for me?" I raise my eyebrows, then scream, "Says the guy who fucked my friend."

"Maybe you should leave before I start airing our dirty laundry," Jagger says.

"Maybe you should stay the fuck out of it. Or are you pissed because you're no longer starting?" Lawrence moves forward. "You should be happy about this, Jordan. Now you can take his spot on the field."

"Careful, Pretty Boy. Wouldn't want to fuck up your throwing arm before the season starts," Jordan says.

"Okay. Everyone stop." I step forward and stand between the three of them. I look up at Lawrence. "You need to leave. Now." I look at Jagger on my other side. "You need to stay out of this."

"I'm not staying out of it." Jagger glares at Lawrence.

"You're still pining after her. After all this time." Lawrence chuckles, shaking his head. "Wow."

Jagger steps forward, right into my palm, which I'm holding up and I know won't do any good if he decides to charge at Lawrence, and from the way his chest is flexing against my hand, I have a feeling he's really trying hard to rein it in right now.

"Please leave." I shut my eyes, heart hammering. This can turn ugly quickly and I don't want this on my already full conscience. "All of you. Please."

Jagger backs away first. My eyes pop open and I see him walking away with Jordan. I let my hands fall at my sides and take a deep breath.

"See you at home, Jo," Jagger says with a snicker as he turns around and walks toward a gray car that must be Jordan's.

"I can't believe you moved in with him," Lawrence says behind me.

"It's none of your fucking business who I move in with or what I do. Are we clear on that?" I raise an eyebrow. "Leave me alone." I walk back to my car and drive away before he says another word.

The entire ride home, I'm shaking so hard that I consider pulling over, but I don't and amongst everything running through my head are Lawrence's words. *You're still pining after her. After all this time.* What the hell did he mean by that? He can't possibly think Jagger likes me. Right?

Chapter Ten

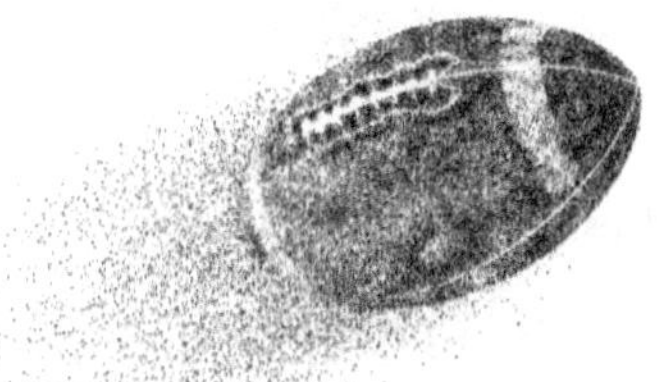

Jagger

I DIDN'T WANT TO COME TO THE BARBECUE, BUT MY BROTHERS started calling me early this morning and showed up to pick me up and drag me along. What I wanted to do was talk to Jo about last night. I thought I'd have a chance when I got up, but her room was wide open and the house was empty, so I assume she left early this morning. I can't even text her since I no longer have her number, the result of a decision I made on a drunken night when I decided I couldn't have it in my phone and not call or text.

The gate that surrounds the Canó house is open when we get there, so Mitch pulls up and parks along the side, where we have easy access to leave whenever we want. We start walking toward the house and spot Carolina Blue balloons leading to the yard and follow them. I've only been to this barbecue once, my freshman year. That year, I was dragged here by my parents.

This year, Mitchell used the excuse that he'd be gone most of the fall since he's going to train with one of the best baseball trainers in the country and take his classes online while he's gone, which means we won't be able to hang out as often. I took the bait like an idiot because I love hanging out with my brothers. I especially love hanging out with Mitch, who's my Irish twin, and therefore, has always been closest to me.

"Boys!" That's Rosa Canó's greeting when she sees us from the other side of their enormous backyard.

She's all wide smile and open arms. She has the complete opposite of Josephine's reaction to me and most things in life, even if they do look like carbon copies of each other, with their olive complexion, dark curls, and beautiful hazel almond-shaped eyes. They have the kind of face that you can't look away from, beautiful and expressive. Mrs. Canó has a bangin' body too, not that I'm trying to check her out or anything, but she usually wears dresses that hug her curves and hit just below the knee. Today, she's wearing khaki pants and a white blouse though. Still, total MILF. Not that I'd ever fuck her. I mean, I hooked up with her daughter for God's sake. The mother-daughter thing is more of Maverick's speed, not mine, and definitely not Mitchell's. She gives each of us a warm hug and firm kiss on the cheek when we reach her, then holds us by the arms and gives us a once-over like a proud mother.

"You are just so handsome." She smiles. "I'm so happy to have you here. You know, I told your mother you could stay here, but she insisted the three of you had places to live. We have plenty of space." She waves a hand at the mansion behind her.

"Thanks for the offer," Mitch says, "but you definitely don't want Maverick living with you. Even Jagger won't room with him."

"Is that so?" She laughs, looking at me.

"He's too messy." I smile, looking around. "Where's Henry?"

"He's barbecuing right over there." She points to the other side of the pool, where I see a very animated Dr. Henry Canó flipping burgers with one hand and holding a cold *Presidente* in the other. "Grab a beer, go mingle. The point of this barbecue is to meet new people. There are coaches and professors and parents and new students. I'm sure they'll all be wanting to talk to three star athletes." Rosa winks and walks away.

"Man, I miss Mom," Maverick says beside me.

"Me too," I sigh.

"Same," Mitch agrees.

"Yo, does Rosa know you're living with Jo?" Mav asks, turning to me.

"Hell no she doesn't know," Mitchell says. "She would have said something."

"You know how they are." I shrug a shoulder. "They're so strict I'm surprised Jo and Misty are allowed out of the house."

"They can't be that strict still," Mitch says.

"No? Why'd you sneak around with Misty when you were together that summer?" I raise an eyebrow at him.

"That's different. We were teenagers. We're adults now."

"You think Ma thinks I'm an adult?" Maverick asks. "She

freaking sent a cleaning lady and had food delivered to me every day last week."

"That's because you're a fucking baby." I shoot him a look. "Neither of us got that treatment."

"Speak for yourself," Mitch snickers. "I put a stop to it quick though."

"Yeah, when the cleaning lady caught you fucking that cheerleader," I said.

"Right." Mitch chuckles. "Damn, that was embarrassing."

"You shouldn't have given her a key to your place, dummy," Mav adds. Mitch shrugs a shoulder.

"I never got a cleaning lady." I frown.

"That's because you're a control freak. Ma knows better than to send you anything. She'd never hear the end of it," Mav says. "It must be firstborn syndrome because I definitely don't understand it."

"No, you don't." I grin. Mav shakes his head.

"Let's grab a beer. You know the *Presidente*'s are dressed like brides here, as Dad would say." Mitch winks, switching from English to Spanish half-way through the sentence. My brother always turns up his Dominican slang when we're around other Dominicans and I can't help but to laugh as we make our way in the direction of Dr. Canó.

When we reach him, he sets the burger he's grilling on a plate, along with the spatula. He opens his arms wide and grins at us. Henry Canó is a big man. He's a former baseball player himself, who could have absolutely gone to the majors like Dad, but he tore a ligament early on in his minor league career and decided to hang up his cleats and pursue a degree in medicine. Dad respects him more than he respects anyone else in the world. He always says Henry knew what he was doing when he walked away from the game and that he's the most successful person he knows, despite Dad making a lot more money than him. We grew up thinking of Henry as some sort of god, and him being all of our godfather meant we saw him pretty often before we settled in New York for good and the Canós settled down in the middle of North Carolina, something I never understood, as a city guy.

"Well, would you look at what the cat dragged in," he boasts, brown eyes dancing. "My dudes. Damn you're huge. When did this happen?"

"Mav just passed dad in height this summer and never leaves the gym." I go in for a hug and pull away so my brothers can do the same.

"Wow." He shakes his head, looking at the three of us with a chuckle. "This is wild." He looks over at Mitch. "I didn't expect you to be here."

"My training starts next week." Mitch smiles.

"Are you excited about it? I bet you are."

"I think Dad's more excited than I am," Mitch says with a laugh. "But yeah, I mean, I couldn't pass up the opportunity."

"There's a lot of talks about you going to the majors. How are you feeling about it?" Henry asks.

"I feel like I don't want to jinx anything." Mitch shrugs. "Carson signed this summer."

"You could have signed as well," I point out.

"Eh." Mitch cocks his head as if he's not so sure. Henry looks at me and shrugs a shoulder.

My brother doesn't like talking about it much because as he says, he doesn't want to jinx anything, but I get a feeling there's a lot more to it. He's had a few opportunities and passed on them for different reasons. I'm not one to judge, but it drives me crazy to see someone I know can succeed actually take a chance on it. Deep down, I think he's constantly comparing himself to dad. I guess in a way we all are, but Mav and I don't play baseball, so even though we live in our father, the man's shadow, we don't live in our father, the baseball god's shadow. Mitch does.

"That's the one you introduced me to during your last game last season?" Henry asks, taking the spotlight away from my obviously uncomfortable brother.

"Yep. The short stop. He's going to play for the Astros now."

"Amazing. You do you, Mitchell. Don't worry about everyone else." Henry smiles, then looks over at me and gets serious. "Why haven't you come to see me? Your father said your shoulder is still acting up."

"I was planning on going soon." I glance down briefly because I hate being under his scrutinizing gaze. "Coach said—"

"I don't care what your coach said. Tell him you're coming to the practice to do physical therapy from now on, every week. If you want to see the field again, you need to stay on top of this."

"Dad's dying for him to switch to baseball. Coach Wallace said he'd put him straight on the roster, but you know these guys with their football and hockey dreams." Mitch rolls his eyes with a chuckle. "I mean seriously, how many Dominicans that you know play hockey?"

"This is America, Mitch. That means we can do whatever the hell we want. The only reason dad played baseball was that it was the only sport available to him." I reach for three beers in the cooler beside us and hand one to each of my brothers. "Besides, the adrenaline isn't the same in baseball."

"I think he's fine right where he is." Henry takes a swig of his beer and looks around. "Have you met any of the people here? There are a lot of former players, not that you don't meet great athletes all the time, but these people are from your alma mater."

"We just got here," Mav says. "I'm definitely looking forward to seeing some basketball players."

"Walk around. There's food on the tables over there. You already know to make yourselves at home." Henry takes some hot dogs and sets them on the grill. My brothers and I are walking away when he stops me. "Jag. A word please."

"Sure." I nod at my brothers, who are idling around wondering if they should stay behind. Once they start walking away, I turn my attention to Henry.

"What have you been doing for your shoulder?"

"Honestly? Not much." I take a long sip of beer. "I was doing therapy in New York, but . . . " I glance away momentarily, hoping to avert the situation but knowing it'll be impossible.

"Don't you want to heal your shoulder?"

"Of course." When I meet his eyes, he's watching me closely.

"So come by the practice."

"I have to see when I have time to with classes and—"

"Come by on Monday after five. It'll be closed by then, but I'll be able take a look at it myself and see what I can do."

"I can't ask you to stay there late for me."

"You didn't ask me to do that." He raises an eyebrow. "I'm telling you to do it."

I nod, because there's no way out of this. Henry is like a brother to my father and they speak often enough that if I don't go to his practice he'll mention it to my father, who's been telling me to go over there since I got here.

"Go. Enjoy yourself." He nods toward the lawn. "I'll see you Monday."

"See you Monday." I smile and walk away and join my brothers, who are already talking to a group of guys.

Chapter Eleven

Jagger

WE'RE THERE LONG ENOUGH FOR ME TO GET A SECOND BEER before Josephine opens the door to the back of the house. She's wearing a jean mini skirt that show off her long, defined legs, a white T-shirt that's tied up and shows off just a bit of her toned stomach, and checkered Vans. I know most guys want to see women in lingerie or naked, but she is my literal wet dream. My heart skips a beat at the sight of her, and it's because of it that I look away, trying to pay attention to the conversation going on in front of me. I think they're still comparing Lebron to Jordan, but I can't be sure. When Steph Curry comes up in conversation, I know I'm definitely far behind. Still, better to pretend I'm paying attention than look over at Jo again.

"Damn, she's hot." My eyes snap up to the guy across from me who spoke the words. He's on the hockey team. A junior who said he's not finishing the year because he'll be drafted in November. All eyes follow to see where he's looking and sure enough, it's Josephine.

"She's like a sister to us," Mav says, making a face.

Mitch shoots me a smirk as he takes a sip of beer. I shoot him a look that says *don't mess with me right now*. He looks away with the same damn smirk. Jo may be one of our oldest friends, but she's never been like a sister to me. Or maybe she was before I noticed how damn pretty she was, but that was four years ago and I haven't stopped wanting her since. I can't stand it sometimes. I can't stand *her* most times. Not because she's not cool or funny or straight up hot as hell, but because I genuinely thought there was something more between us before she started dating Lawrence. Then again, I thought he was my friend before he went behind my back and started going after her. It wouldn't even bother me if I hadn't told him I had my eye on her. Some would say the fault is mine for not moving fast enough. I still think he's an asshole.

"I'd ask her out, but I'm scared of Dr. Canó." The guy wiggles his eyebrows. "Maybe I'll ask her to come to my draft party, you know what I'm sayin'?"

"Maybe you should do whatever you think you're going to do before November," another guy says. "She just broke up with Lawrence."

"Damn that bastard. I knew he was cheating on her, but I didn't realize how bad it was," guy number one says. "I just don't understand who would cheat on *that*."

"An idiot," guy number two says.

I can't disagree with them there, but I finish off my beer and walk away. Standing by while they're fawning over Jo is definitely not my idea of a good time. I toss the glass bottle into the recycling can and look up to see Jo standing in the corner texting furiously. I walk over to her, reminding myself that no one will think anything of this. We've known each other since we were kids. We had a lot of firsts together. I cringe inwardly thinking about the last time we actually spent time together before this semester. The party we bumped into each other at was wild, to say the least, and things got out of hand faster than I anticipated. We'd both been drinking, but we weren't drunk. We couldn't blame the alcohol for what we did. For years I've played the scenario over in my head. For years I've thought about and fantasized what it would be like having her underneath me again. For years I've tried just as hard to block it out, especially when I find myself on the field playing against Lawrence, but most of the time in those situations I wish I played defense instead of offense, because I would love to light his ass up once and for all. I take a breath when I'm almost at her side and remind myself to stop being an asshole and start being nice. It's the only way I can fix what happened and the only way we'll survive rooming together.

Chapter Twelve

Jo

I'M PUTTING MY PHONE IN THE BACK POCKET OF MY SKIRT WHEN Jagger sidles up beside me. My heart skips a beat unwillingly even before I glance over and see that he's wearing khakis and a short sleeve button-down. I swear the man makes everything look good.

"I hate this party. I always skip it," I say, leaving out the part where I always skip it because I always go to Duke's mixer that lands on the same day.

"It's all right. Free food, cold beer. I mean, what more can you want?"

"You're such a guy." I snort, shaking my head.

"Can't argue there." He shrugs a shoulder. "So. You haven't told your parents."

"About our living arrangement?" I face him quickly, eyes wide. "No, did you?"

"Of course not." He scowls. "I just don't understand why *you* haven't told them."

"You know why."

"No, I really don't." He says the words slowly, as if to give me an opportunity to mull it over.

I roll my eyes instead. Does he know nothing about my parents? They've always given my sister and me enough freedom to make our own mistakes, but living with a guy before we're married or at least engaged? That would be a huge no-no. They're very traditional in that regard and in a way, so are we. Lawrence asked me to move in with him and I gave him a definitive no. I know living with a Cruz brother would probably set my mother's mind at ease in a sense, because she seems to like them more than she likes Misty and me most days, but still. She was the one who laid down the gauntlet without giving me a chance to explain or redeem myself in regard to the car accident. It was my mother who came up with the idea of me footing the bill for the crashed luxury car and I am not going to give her any news that may be good news. Not if I can help it.

"They'd make it a huge deal," I say finally. "Also, me rooming with a guy? My mom would have a heart attack."

"I don't think you're giving your mom enough credit. We're not living together in a romantic way. We're roommates."

"Yes, I know." I look away from him and out to the party. When I spot his brothers, who are looking at us along with the two guys they're talking to, I smile and wave at them before turning back to the least nice Cruz brother. "We also share a bathroom."

"I'm well aware. We've been living together for two days and you already clogged up the shower with your hair."

"I did not." My face pulls. "I pick up my hair after I wash it."

"Yet it was clogging the drain." He raises an eyebrow. "Don't worry, I took care of it."

I cross my arms. Jagger loves to get the last word in and I'm going to let him. The last couple of years of dating a popular football player, I've learned to pick my battles. Some people are just too competitive for their own good.

"The point is, I'm not going to tell them about our living arrangement."

"That's fine." He shrugs a shoulder. "It's not like I'm going around announcing it to the world."

"Good."

"Sure." I shrug a shoulder back, keeping my arms crossed. "Are you sticking around?"

"Probably not. Misty texted that she's not coming and I'm over athletes."

"You're over athletes?" He chuckles. "Aren't you an athlete?"

"*Was.*"

"What happened with that?" He turns to face me fully, genuine interest in his eyes. "UNC is a D1 school. You had to be great to be on the team."

"I guess." I turn away slightly.

The last thing I want is to get into this conversation, but if I know one thing about Jagger it's that he won't drop it. He'll either run me down today or tomorrow or the next day but he will get to the bottom of it one way or another.

"So, what happened?"

"I don't want to talk about it."

"I know I'm not the only one asking you this."

"What happened to your shoulder?" I meet his gaze. "Are you getting back on the field this season?"

"Fair." His lips purse and he turns away.

I'm about to open my mouth to apologize because I didn't mean it to sound that . . . mean . . . but I decide not to. He would have kept picking at my sore had I not fired that question at him, so I shouldn't need to be any different. After a few moments, I decide to leave. I don't want to stand there with Jagger and I definitely don't want to speak to anyone at the party, especially now. If people are going to start asking me why I'm not playing volleyball, I may end up losing my shit and crying the rest of the afternoon and I'm not up for it. As it is, I'm emotionally spent from it all. I don't need more reminders about how royally I fucked up my life.

Chapter Thirteen

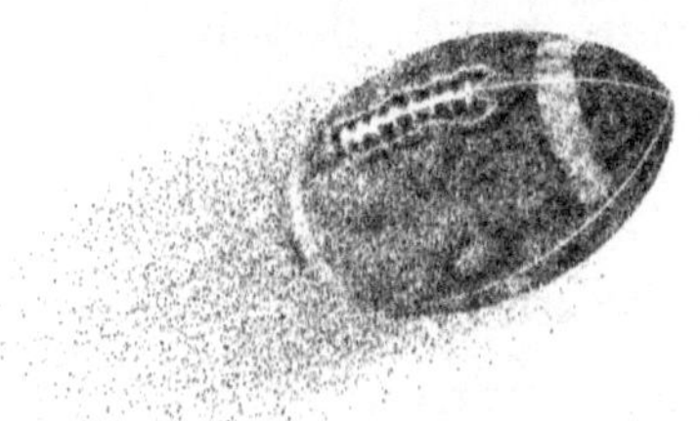

Jo

'M WIPING DOWN THE LAST TABLE WHEN THE DOORS OPEN AGAIN. Without glancing up, I say, "We're closed. Sorry," and curse Marissa for not locking the doors.

"Can we talk?" The sound of Lawrence's voice makes me jump up and whip my attention to the front door.

"Seriously?"

"I missed you at the barbecue today," he says.

"I didn't miss going."

"Jo." He sighs heavily.

"I don't want to talk, Lawrence. You've said and done enough. Can't you just leave me alone?"

"Coach wants me to ask you . . ." He steps forward tentatively and I notice he's holding a paper in his hand. "I swear I didn't come up with this idea."

"What is that?" I eye him and the paper.

"Coach thinks you should sign this NDA."

"NDA?" I blink. "You're kidding me."

"They're going to draft me after this season and I have to tie up loose ends."

"Loose ends?" I scoff. "I'm a loose end?"

"No." He takes another step forward. "I mean, according to him, yes."

"Do I look like a person who wants revenge?" I search his blue eyes. It's crazy how I thought he was so damn hot before. He still is, but now that I know he's also a cheater and a liar and a manipulator I no longer find him attractive. "If I wanted revenge, I would have keyed your car or slashed your tires or something."

"I think he's afraid you'll speak to reporters." He flinches as he says the words and that and the way he's cowering are the only signs that the man I once loved is still in there somewhere.

"Let me see the paper." I yank it from his hand when he extends it to me. It's basically a one-page summary of all the things I can't do if I sign it—speak about Lawrence in a bad light, write a tell-all book, I snort-laugh at that one and look at him. "As if you're so interesting that anyone will want to read a tell-all book about you."

"Can you please just sign it?"

I hold a finger up to silence him and keep reading. My heart hammers when I read the last point in the contract. The one that says I will not go to the authorities or university with any information that may defame his character.

"I need to think this over." I fold the page in half and look up at him. "When do you need it signed by?"

"Preferably by the end of the week. I mean, really he wants it done tonight, but I can stall."

"I just . . . I need a moment."

"I understand." He swallows. "I truly am sorry, Jo."

"So you've said."

"I'll pay you. Whatever you want, I'll pay you once I sign my NFL contract."

"I don't want your money." I scowl. "I don't want anything from you. Don't you get that?"

"I do. And I'm sorry. I'm sorry for everything."

I nod and bite the inside of my cheek to keep from reacting to his apology. I walk him to the door and lock it after he leaves. Somehow, I'm able to finish cleaning and get in my car before I completely lose it, sobbing uncontrollably. I once saw my mother crying in the driveway. Really crying. So much that I thought someone had died. I ran down the stairs and waited for her in the kitchen, heart in my throat, fully expecting her to say that when she walked in. Instead, she smiled wide and gave me a hug as if nothing happened, as if she hadn't been crying hysterically out in the driveway. I never asked her about it, but I think about it a lot these days, when I find that the only refuge I really have is this beat-up old car with no functioning radio.

When I pull up to the house and park, I notice there are two cars there. One belongs to Jagger and the other is a white Lexus I've never seen. I wipe my face and take a breath as I walk up the walkway and up the steps. If he's in his room with a woman tonight I think I'll scream. Then again, if he's in his room with someone, it would mean he'd leave me alone. Still, there's a nagging feeling sitting in the pit of my stomach as I unlock the front door. When I open the door, I'm greeted by Jagger, Jordan from the other night, and three girls I've never seen before. Two of them are sidled up next to Jagger while he leans forward on the couch, completely ignoring them and keeping his eyes on the Madden game he's playing. Another girl is on the other couch beside Jordan, with her legs on his as he also plays the game and ignores her. "Hey," Jordan says, looking up at me momentarily.

"Hey." I look at him, then at Jagger, then the three girls.

"Hi," two of them say. I give a wave. Jagger ignores me completely.

"We have a few slices of pizza left," Jordan says. "Pepperoni."

"Thanks." I feel myself smile a little even though he's no longer looking at me and I'm already moving to the kitchen and out of their line of vision.

I open the fridge and am pleasantly surprised with how organized it is. Jagger lined up all of the sodas, sports drinks, beer, and water. He also put everything away in a way that's easy to find, from vegetables to fruits. I grab a bottle of water and open the pantry to see it's in the same shape as the fridge. I grab a handful of cashews and a banana from the counter. I start eating the cashews because I hate taking things like that to my room.

"What the fuck," Jordan screams, while Jagger laughs. "Damn you. I thought I had you that time. I'm gonna go outside to smoke."

"I'll come with," one girl says.

"Do you have anything to drink besides water?" another asks.

"Let's pre-game before the party," another says.

"Shit. At what time is the party?" Jordan asks.

I walk to my room as they discuss whatever party it is they're going to. Hopefully they're going somewhere and it's not a party that Jagger decided to have here without consulting me. Honestly, even if he somehow decided to pull that, I don't care. I'm spent. I'd probably sleep through it anyway. I'm pushing my door open when I see Jagger walking in my direction, his light brown eyes taking me in and zoning on my face.

"What happened to you?"

"Huh?" I push my door open and walk in, setting my snacks down on my nightstand along with the folded-up white paper I've been holding on to since I saw Lawrence. "What do you mean?"

"Did something happen?" Jagger asks behind me.

"How would you know? It's not like you even bothered to look at me when I got here or say hello like a cordial human being. Your mother would not be pleased."

"At least my mother knows I'm living with you."

"You told her?" I gasp, turning to face him quickly.

"Of course I told her. Don't worry, she won't tell Rosa."

"Right." I scoff. "Because they don't gossip all the time."

"I asked her not to tell your mother and she won't."

"Okay."

"Are you going to tell me what's wrong?" He searches my eyes and for a moment I think there may be a flicker of concern in his before I look away. Instead of answering, I gather my pajamas and underwear and brush past him, locking myself in the bathroom. Even with the door between us I can see the shadow of his feet on the other side of the door. "Some privacy, please," I call out.

"You act like I walked in there with you."

"No, but you're standing on the other side and I need to pee."

"Performance problems?" I hear the smirk in his voice and roll my eyes.

"Don't you have a video game to play? Girls to screw? Whatever it is you were planning on doing before I walked in the house."

He doesn't answer, but he does step away from the door and I go back to doing my business. Instead of just washing my hands and going back to my room, I decide to shower. Standing under the spray of warm water always helps me forget my problems. I lose track of how long I'm in there, but when I'm done, I towel dry my hair for a few minutes before getting dressed in my favorite gray cotton shorts and cropped Duke T-shirt. I should get rid of it being that I'm not planning to attend any Duke football games this season, but Misty goes there now so I wear it with pride. I notice Jagger's door is open as well as mine and the television looks like it's off. I assume they left and tip-toe to my room, shutting the door behind me.

"So." Jagger's voice makes me jump.

"What the hell, Jagger?" I whip around to see him sitting at the edge of my bed, watching me with a bemused expression on his face that I want to slap off.

"You took forever. I bet you used up all the hot water."

"What are you doing here?"

"Waiting for you to tell me what's wrong, but I figured it has something to do with this." He taps the paper on my nightstand.

"You're going through my stuff?" I walk forward, snatching the paper from the nightstand and backing away quickly. "Get out of my room. I thought we set boundaries."

"We did." He stands and walks over to me. "I never said I intended to follow them."

"What's the point if you're not going to follow them?" I know I should lower my voice, but I can't. I also can't seem to stop shaking. "I can't believe you went through my things."

"I didn't. I walked in, sat on your bed, and the paper fell. I picked it up and looked at it. I didn't read the entire thing, but I figured it's an NDA for Lawrence."

"You just . . . figured that without reading it?" I shake my head.

"I have the same ones. It's pretty standard."

"Pretty standard." I blink. "It's standard to make

your ex-girlfriend of nearly three years sign a paper that says she won't talk about you?"

"It is now that he's going pro."

"And you? Are you going pro?"

He looks away. It's the third time in my life I've ever seen Jagger look unsure of something. The second was at my parents' barbecue. The first was . . . *that time* that I can't even bring myself to think about without my entire body heating up and me feeling like I need to flee.

"Tell me."

"You tell me first. What's wrong? Are you upset because of this?" He taps the paper in my hand, his gaze on mine again, and I realize we're standing a little too close to each other and we're in my bedroom and something inside me is blooming too fast for me to stomp and kill it.

I nod my head and lick my lips. His eyes clock the movement momentarily before he looks back into my eyes.

"You want to talk about it?"

"No. Do you want to talk about why you're avoiding the conversation about you playing again?"

"No."

"Okay then."

He takes one step closer, his warmth enveloping me quickly. I feel myself take a breath and struggle to let it out with the way he's looking at me. "Unless we trade a secret for a secret?"

"I don't know what you mean," I whisper.

"I think you do." He's so close now I have to tilt my head to keep meeting his eyes.

"Why do you care so much?"

"Because you look like you've been crying and that kills me."

My heart slams into my chest. "Why?"

"I don't know." He lets out a soft breath that tickles my forehead. "I only know what I feel."

"I can't." I swallow and take a step back. "This can't happen."

Roommates. We're roommates. This can't happen. Last time it happened he basically turned his back on me for good and right now I can't handle one more bad thing. Jagger gives one single nod, searches my eyes one last time, and leaves my room, shutting the door softly behind him.

"By the way, burn the shirt you're wearing," he says from the other side of the door. "Or I'll go through your things and burn it myself."

That shouldn't make me laugh. It definitely shouldn't make me feel like my skin is on fire or make me want to open the door and yank him back in here, but all of those things are true. I fight the urge to do the last one though because I know it's a horrible idea to sleep with my roommate, especially when my roommate is Jagger Cruz.

Chapter Fourteen

Jo

I TAKE A SEAT NEAR THE DOOR, A FEW SEATS DOWN FROM THE SEAT Jagger claimed for himself. I left the house extra early today and won't be returning until after I help clean Dad's practice tonight. It's not that I'm avoiding Jagger per se, but I also don't want to run into him right now. I know it's impossible not to face him. We live together, we have this class together, and for some strange reason I can't seem to stop seeing him everywhere. Well, the reason isn't that strange. The last few years I've been able to avoid most people who attend my university because I was so busy hanging out with the Duke kids. Now that I'm here for real, I know it's just a matter of time before I start running into people I'd avoided during that time, like my old teammates, and Jagger. Specifically Jagger Cruz. I'm purposely staring at my phone, texting Misty and asking her inconsequential things like how her night was and whether or not she got into the journalism class she needed. Mostly, I'm avoiding looking up out of fear that I'll see Jagger and he'll see me and I just . . . I need a moment. He almost kissed me last night. He would have if I hadn't pulled away. Part of me is screaming *what is wrong with you?* And the other part knows I'm not ready for that, and even if I was, Jagger Cruz is definitely not the one. He's not. Yes, he's ridiculously good-looking and his body is a work of art. Yes, he's kind and charming and all the things women look for in a man. It doesn't change the fact that he's an athlete and women flock to him, and at the end of the day, he's a man and I generally don't trust men anymore.

When the professor starts speaking, I finally set my phone aside and look up, ready to take notes. In doing so, I inadvertently look around and find that Jagger isn't sitting anywhere near me. He's on the other side of the classroom, in the middle row, with a woman sidled up to his seat. Not a woman. That woman. The one I saw him having sex with that night. I hate the feeling of jealousy that envelops me instantly. I really shouldn't care. I shouldn't. I turned him down last night. Rightfully so. I take a deep breath and focus on the professor, but spend the majority of the class distracted. The girl he's with keeps putting her hand on his arm, on his shoulder, on his thick, unruly hair. I wonder how long they've been hooking up. She's obviously not his girlfriend. I wonder if she wants to be, then snort softly at my own question. Of course she wants to be. They all want to be. It was like that when we were young as well. There were always girls, usually cheerleaders, trying to get with him. With the three Cruz brothers, if I'm being honest. It drove Misty crazy that one summer that she was dating Mitch.

Before I know it, the class is over, and people start heading outside. Because I'm sitting right by the back door, I twist my body so that my feet aren't in the way of anyone walking by as I put away my things in my large crossbody and look for my phone again. As I'm zipping it closed, I look up to see Jagger walking by with the girl. She's pretty up close, a brunette with fair skin and freckles over her nose and cheeks. She doesn't look in my direction, but she's smiling wide and flirtatious as she turns and looks at Jagger who's right behind her. He doesn't look at me either, just keeps his attention on her as she speaks to him. My heart tightens as they walk off. I stand up and walk out, staying far behind them as we head in the same direction, but I can't seem to look away from them. I feel like a stalker, watching them so closely. A legit stalker, because even as they turn toward Lenoir Hall, I turn with them. There's a group of guys who are obviously athletes, and that's where they stop and I keep going. I to go to work anyway. I don't have time to think about my confused feelings.

"Don't worry about the bathrooms tonight," Donna says as she gets up from her desk. "Milton says you did a bad job last time."

"Milton said that?" My mouth falls open. "I did a great job!"

"That's not what he said." Donna laughs. "It doesn't matter. What does matter is that I need you to open the door for someone. I'm celebrating my thirty-eighth anniversary tonight, so your father told me to leave early." She looks at her watch. "I'm already late."

"What door do I open?" I frown.

"The front door, silly. It'll be locked."

"Oh." I look at the front door, then at the clock over the door. "But it's five-oh-five. We're closed. Dad's taking a patient at this time?"

"He is."

"I thought he didn't do that anymore? Mom is going to be so mad."

"He made an exception." Donna shoots me a look. "Now, can I trust you'll do a better job with the door than you did with the toilets?"

"Yes."

"Good." She laughs as she walks away and calls out, "Turn that frown upside down."

"Sure," I mutter and go back to sweeping.

Dad shares the practice with two other doctors. The three of them are the most coveted in orthopedics in the United States. People fly here from all over the country and all over the world to get second opinions and surgeries. Mondays, two out of three are usually out of the office. Today, Dad is the one who happens to be here, which is why he designated me to clean every Monday as penance. I set the broom aside and walk over to his office, knocking on the slightly open door to see if he needs anything and reprimand him for telling someone to come in after hours after he promised he wouldn't go home late anymore.

"Come in."

I open the door a little wider. "Donna said someone is coming in soon."

"That is correct." He looks up from the papers in front of him. "Is that a problem?"

"I thought you weren't going to stay at work late anymore."

"I assure you I ran this by your mother." He raises an amused eyebrow. "Am I in trouble with you?"

"No." I purse my lips to contain a smile. "Do you need anything?"

"Not at the moment. Do you want to help me with rehab?"

"Sure." I shrug a shoulder. "Anything is better than cleaning."

Dad chuckles. "Come back and get me when he arrives. Set him up in room five."

"Got it."

I walk away and go down the hall to room five, switching on the lights and making sure everything else is set up. I'm not an expert by any means, but one room I know well is this physical therapy room. There are five in this practice, all catering to different things. Room five is simple, just a patient bed, a computer screen that takes up one wall that's used to show patients scans, X-rays, and even exercises they should work on at home. It's definitely a state-of-the-art facility that Dad is proud of. I sanitize the patient bed quickly before setting a new strip of paper on it just in case before I hear the buzz of the front door and walk in that direction. I look up at the screen beside the door to see who's outside and freeze momentarily before unlocking the door.

"You have got to be kidding me." I pull the door open. "You're following me here too?"

"Following you?" He huffs out a single laugh. "You think way too highly of yourself if you think you're worth following."

"Well, then, what are you doing here?"

"I have an appointment with your dad."

"You?"

"Yeah." He looks at me like I'm the one who's crazy, and now that I'm taking a step back and letting him walk inside, I realize that all of that probably came off as a little crazy. Not that I'll admit that to him or anyone. I shut the door and lock it behind him before brushing past him and walking in front of him.

"Follow me."

"What are you doing here anyway?" he asks behind me.

"Working."

"You have two jobs?"

"I am capable of working two jobs, you know." I roll my eyes even though he can't see me. I'm not going to tell him that even though I hate cleaning, this is by far the easiest job since it's only once a week. Not that it's a job per se since dad's not paying me for it. It's more like a cleaning internship. I laugh at that.

"What's so funny?"

"Nothing." I stop at room five and open the door, waving a hand for him to step inside. "Why are you here anyway?"

"I injured my left shoulder last season." He says it like the mere words leave a bad taste in his mouth and looks at me like I'm at fault.

"Oh."

"So, what do I do?" He looks around the room.

"Just wait here. I'll go get him." I walk out of the room and jog over to Dad's office, knocking once before opening the door. "He's in room five."

"Perfect." Dad looks back down at the paper in front of him. "Do me a favor, have him take his shirt off, and power up the computer. I'm going to send you a file that I need opened on the big screen."

"Okay." I walk out and jog over to room five, coming to a dead stop when I fully realize what my dad just asked me to do and who I'm supposed to ask to do this. "Um . . . " I bite my lip.

"What?" Jagger turns to face me.

"I need you to take your shirt off."

He chuckles. "Okay."

I give a nod and walk over to the computer, turning it on. I'm trying really hard not to watch Jagger do as instructed, but it's impossible and not because he's hot or anything. He seems to be struggling with the task. After a few seconds of hearing him huffing and sighing, I stand up and look at him.

"You can't take your shirt off?"

"I practiced today," he says.

"Okay?" I blink.

"My shoulder's tight."

"Okay," I say with a little more confusion.

"I need help, okay?"

"Taking off your shirt?" I squeak.

"Yes." He glances down at his sneakers. "Look, this is uncomfortable for me too."

"Having a woman take your shirt off makes you uncomfortable?"

"No." He glances up quickly, shooting me a dirty look. "Obviously not."

"Having me do it makes you uncomfortable?" I frown.

"Well, we're not exactly doing this for recreation, Josephine. This is about my fucked-up shoulder, so yes." He's shooting daggers at me.

Rather than saying anything back, I walk over and reach for the hem of his black cotton T-shirt. I start lifting it slowly, my fingers brushing against his warm, tight skin, unable to ignore the defined V or perfect six-pack underneath it as I uncover each inch of skin. I swallow when I reach his chest and pause there since I know this is the part that's uncomfortable for his shoulder. I meet his gaze and find him staring at me, expression dark and smoldering.

"I'm trying not to hurt you," I whisper.

He doesn't say a word, but he doesn't look away from me as he tucks his healthy arm out of the right sleeve, leaving the shirt bunched up against his neck and his left sleeve still on. I reach up and he ducks slightly to help me pull it over his head, the movement putting me nose to nose with him. My heart is hammering so loudly now I can barely think let alone breathe correctly.

"Focus, Josephine," he whispers.

I nod, my nose brushing against his as I finish pulling his shirt off his other arm and take a step back just as my father's footsteps get closer and he walks in the room.

"You're late," Dad says behind me and even though I knew he just walked in, I jump to the other side of the room, still holding Jagger's shirt in my hand. "Next week you have to be on time. I can't stay late every week."

"It won't happen again. I was stuck explaining to Coach why I wasn't going to use the team's PT."

"Coach?" Dad raises an eyebrow, then looks over at me, then at Jagger. "You went to practice?"

"I did."

"Did you just have my daughter help you take off your shirt?"

"Yes." Jagger clears his throat.

"Which means you can't do a simple task on your own," Dad says. "Which means you shouldn't have been practicing today. What the hell are your coaches thinking?"

"I told them I was fine."

"You told them you were fine and they listened?" Dad shakes his head. "Pull up the file I sent, Josephine."

I click the file and watch as a ton of different X-ray pictures pop up on my screen and the big screen beside me. I click the first one. I know I'm looking at a shoulder, but I have no idea what to look for in an X-ray, so I don't even try. I set Jagger's T-shirt down beside me and click on the next picture and the next as Dad instructs me.

"It's still healing," Dad says finally. "He did a great job pushing it back in place. Have you been doing the exercises he recommended?"

"Not really."

"Have you been laying off the weights?"

"For the most part."

"For the most part," Dad says. "Do you want to get back on the field or not?"

"Of course I do."

"You're not acting like it." Dad shoots him a hard look.

Once he finishes looking at the pictures, he goes over exercises with Jagger, winding motions, him standing with his back against the wall and bringing his arms up to a v-position. They do five different exercises that seem fairly easy but all make Jagger hiss out in pain. I feel kind of bad for him. When they're done, Dad pats Jagger's arm, rubs antibacterial gel on his hands, and tells him to come back next week. As he's walking out, he glances at me.

"Can I trust you to lock up tonight? Your mother's been waiting for me."

"Sure."

"Finish sweeping the floors. I'll know if you don't."

"Okay."

"Don't even worry about the bathrooms. Milton said—"

"I know, Dad. Donna already told me." I shake my head and look away.

"Well, Josephine, I don't think I need to explain to you why you're here, do I? Because if you need me to go over the things you've done wrong and the lapse of judgment—"

"I'm good, Dad," I mutter, keeping my eyes on the ground, wishing I could totally disappear from earth in this moment. "Thank you for letting me pay you back and stuff."

"You're welcome." He walks out.

Jagger is still standing there, but thankfully hasn't spoken a word. I'm pretty sure if he does or says something nice I'll start crying right on the spot. I give myself a count of ten before taking a nice deep breath, shutting down the computer, and grabbing Jagger's shirt. I toss it to him as I walk out of the room.

"I'll be in the hall." I turn around and start walking out.

"I need help putting it back on."

"Are you freaking kidding me?" I pivot around and walk over to him, grabbing the shirt from his hand. I avoid eye contact as I help him slide his left arm into the sleeve, put the neck over his head, and step away. "You really should not be practicing right now."

"I could have put it on myself." He grins.

My jaw drops. "That's not funny."

"I beg to differ." He finishes putting on his T-shirt and I turn around and walk into the hall, picking up the broom to continue cleaning.

"You want help?"

"No, thank you." I focus on the floor.

"You sure? I don't mind."

I stop sweeping and look at him. "You can't even put your shirt on. You think you can help me sweep?"

"I have my right arm. You'd be surprised at the things I can still do."

"I'm good." I shake my head, fighting a blush and dirty thoughts. "Really. If Dad caught wind that I let someone help me with this . . . " I shake my head. As it is, his words caused a lump in my throat that I haven't yet gotten rid of and I need Jagger to leave before I can cry in peace.

"You want company?"

"Nope."

"Okay." He shrugs his right shoulder. "See you around then, Roomie."

I don't even watch him leave. I'm so pissed off and sad at what my dad said and Lawrence's stupid NDA and those are the only things that get me through my angry sweeping session. The last thing I need is to focus on Jagger Cruz and his kindness and his gorgeous face or his stupid muscles.

surgery that Wednesday." Misty rolls her eyes. "I swear he's a workaholic."

"Well, him being a workaholic affords us some pretty cool stuff. Like that Chanel bag." I jut my chin toward the black bag on the bar.

"This was a graduation present, thank you very much."

"Yeah, because all high school graduates are given a freaking four-thousand-dollar present."

"You got a car." She raises an eyebrow.

"Which *you're* currently driving."

"Only because you decided to get a DUI while driving and then crashing a freaking Maserati, Jo." She shakes her head. "I seriously always thought I'd be the one to screw up big, but that's kind of unattainable on the level of screw-ups."

"I know. You don't need to remind me."

"Dad literally spent as much money as he spent on this bag to make sure your record would be expunged, so technically you could have gotten one of these bags too, maybe even two of them."

"Okay. I get it." I swallow. The door that leads to the kitchen opens and we both snap our heads to see Uncle Adrian walking through.

"Hey. My favorite nieces." He walks over and pulls me into a quick hug before reaching over and tapping Misty on the head once. "You finally decided to get smart and have lunch here instead of spending your money elsewhere."

"Yeah, but unless you want me to have a heart attack by

age forty, I'll probably go back to my overpriced green shakes and acai bowls."

"You trying to say my food is unhealthy?" He raises an eyebrow. "Don't let your grandmother hear you talking like that. She loves Lucia's food."

"Oh, Nana knows," I say. "Why do you think she never invites Misty to dinner anymore?"

"She invites me." Misty frowns.

"No, she doesn't." I smile.

"So, listen, Maverick Cruz is here now, and your father wanted to do a proper welcome party for him since he did it for Jagger and Mitchell," Uncle Adrian says. "I'm going to need you to close up now and come back at five."

"Tonight?"

"Yep." He glances over at Misty. "I would love it if you could help. It'll be easy, just setting plates in front of people and picking them up. The bar will be open, but they'll have to come up to get their own drinks if they want anything besides water."

"I can't help." Misty's eyes widen. "I mean, I can't."

"Why not? It's eleven-thirty. If you're sitting here, I'm assuming you don't have class today."

"I don't."

"So what's keeping you busy?" Uncle Adrian raises an eyebrow, but before my sister can even think of an answer, he says, "I need you here tonight, Mist. Have I ever asked you for a favor?"

"No."

"Okay, then. Be here at five. Oh, and pick up Grandma while you're at it."

"Me?" Misty blinks. "Why do I have to pick her up?"

"You're the one with the better car."

"Yeah, but I live all the way across town. It only makes sense if Jo picks her up. Besides, Jo's her favorite."

"I'll do it," I say, because I don't mind picking up my grandmother and I really am her favorite.

"She's going to hate that damn Celica," Uncle Adrian says.

"Well, tough luck. I hate the damn Celica and I drive it every day."

"Fair enough. I'll call her and let her know to be ready by four-thirty." He walks back into the kitchen.

"I can't believe this. Mitch will probably be here," Misty says.

"Probably, but who cares?" I shrug a shoulder. "You can't avoid him forever."

"Right."

When I walk into the house, I hear a woman's laughter, which is weird since Jagger's car isn't even parked outside. Maybe he parked down the block and I didn't see it? As I set my keys down beside the door and slip off my sneakers, I hear a door open and the woman's laughter gets louder, then stops completely as I glance up and meet her gaze. It's the one from our math class.

The one from the other night. I feel my cheeks burn as I glance away just as Jagger walks out of the room, pulling on a T-shirt.

"You're the roommate," she says, smiling as we walk by each other. "I think I've seen you on campus."

"Finite Math," I say.

"Oh. Right. I'm Jessa." She smiles giving a little wave.

"Josephine."

"Josephine," she repeats, taking me in slowly. "I like that. It suits you."

"Okay. Thanks. It was nice to meet you." I wave at her and walk toward my bedroom, completely ignoring Jagger who's standing there as well. For some reason, I can't even look at him right now.

As I open my bedroom, I glance over my shoulder to his open bedroom and see the rumpled and messy bedsheets. There's a weird feeling in the pit of my stomach as I open my door and shut it behind me. I give myself a moment, leaning against the door and breathing in and out a few times. *I don't even like Jagger like that, so why is it that every time I see him with a woman I feel like I'm being punched in the gut?* After a few seconds, I push off the door, sit on the bed, and pull up my math homework, which I find surprisingly easy. When I finish, I pick up my phone and scroll social media. I've been lurking for months. Since the accident. Since I got kicked off the volleyball team and my parents acted like disowning me might actually be a better solution to deal with or not deal with the outcome of the embarrassment I caused. I almost hit like on Kelsey's picture, but decide not to. My teammates, the girls who always said they had my back, abandoned me after the accident. Maybe Coach told them to distance themselves. Maybe they decided to do it on their own. Still, it hurts. I have my sister and I love her to pieces, but I miss my friends. Just as I'm setting my phone down, it vibrates.

Misty: What do I wear? All black?

Me: I guess. He didn't say otherwise.

Misty: I hate this. I don't want to go.

Me: If you don't go, you'll get in trouble.

Misty: I'm almost 21, wtf.

Me: I'm 22, yet here I am . . .

Misty: ugh. Whatever. See you later.

I set my phone down for the last time and start getting ready for tonight's event, which I am now dreading as much as my sister.

Chapter Sixteen

Jo

"**W**HAT'S WRONG?"

"Nothing." I look at Jagger, who's in the kitchen eating a bowl of Fruity Pebbles. "Why do you always think something is wrong with me?"

"Because you always have a look on your face that says something is wrong with you."

"That's just my face." I roll my eyes. "I'm fine."

He eyes me up and down. "You showered and changed into the same outfit?"

"This is a different outfit, but thanks for pointing out that no one will notice that I tried to look presentable."

He chuckles. "I didn't say you didn't look presentable."

"Right." I open the fridge and grab a water bottle and a Greek yogurt. "We're running low on supplies already, which is baffling."

"Baffling?" His eyes dance with amusement. "You've obviously never lived with a guy."

"That or maybe your friends who keep coming over should start pitching in to our grocery fund."

"Or I can just pay for the groceries." He shrugs a shoulder.

"Right. I forget. Your mom probably sends you money every week."

"My mom?" He laughs loudly. "Hell no. I have scholarship money."

"To pay for school." I stop opening my yogurt and look up at him. "I thought you declined the sports scholarship and decided to give that money to someone else who needed it? That's what Dad said. Did you get two scholarships?"

"Yep." He grins. "You're not the only one who can be a nerd, you know?"

"Hm." I eye him curiously. "You shouldn't be allowed to be a nerd."

"Because I'm a jock?"

"Yeah." *And hot. And funny. And gorgeous. And nice.* All things I'd never admit aloud. I focus on my yogurt again.

"So you're heading out already?"

"My uncle wants us there at five."

"It's four."

"And he wants me to pick up my grandmother on my way there."

"Doña Sabrina is coming?" Jagger raises an eyebrow. "I haven't seen her in a while."

"Well, she'll be there."

"Is she making cheesecake?"

"Maybe." I purse my lips.

"Damn, I can't wait. Maybe I should go get ready and get there early so I can try some before my brothers eat it all."

I laugh. "I'll save you a slice."

"You promise?"

I meet his gaze and nearly drop my spoon with the way he's looking at me, with an intensity I've only seen in his expression a handful of times, like he's asking me for more than just a slice of cheesecake. I make myself swallow the bit of yogurt I'd put in my mouth and nod as I turn around and throw away the empty container. I need to leave. I'm starting to feel like a coward, always running away from him when I can't handle the emotions he's eliciting, but I am and he is. I call out "see you later" from the door just before I shut it behind me and walk to my car quickly. It's not like he's going to follow me or anything, but I still feel like I'm in a rush to leave.

"Ay, this car is awful," my grandmother says, sucking her teeth.

"Yeah, but it transports me from point A to point B."

"Until it breaks down." She sucks her teeth again. "Does it have a functioning radio?"

"No."

"No?" She gasps, shaking her head. "Jesus, Josephine."

"Nana, you don't even drive. Your judgment is beneath me right now."

"Beneath you where? On the street I feel scraping against my butt every time you go over a median?"

I groan. She's such a pain in the ass, my grandmother, but I love her and I've always loved her way of telling it like it is. Misty gets that trait from her. Mom says it's an Aquarius thing. I don't understand much about astronomy signs, but I know I'm an Aries and most of the things Walter Mercado used to say about us are true. On that note, I turn and glance at my grandmother briefly. She's looking at herself in the little mirror behind her sun visor, fixing the red lipstick she's wearing. She always tries to get me to wear it because we have similar complexions—olive skin with dark hair—but whenever I wear lipstick I feel like a clown.

"Did you see the Walter Mercado special on Netflix?" I ask.

"Not yet." She sighs. "I got sucked into another Spanish show. Let me tell you, those Spaniards can tell a story and hook you. I wish I'd known that before. To think I wasted all of those years on telenovelas." She purses her lips and shakes her head as she pats the coils of short curls on her head.

"You love your telenovelas, Nan." I shoot her a sideways glance.

"I'm done with them."

"You say that every time." I laugh. "Remember when we met that actor at the vet and you almost forgot your dog there because you were so enamored?"

"Fernando Colunga. How could I forget?" She smiles. "I don't know why your father chose to move out of Miami and land in the middle of nowhere North Carolina," she says with distaste.

"To be fair, Uncle Adrian was here first."

"Yes, but who follows Adrian? Only an idiot would."

"Yet, here we are." I laugh again. "You have to admit, it's nice here, and we have the seasons."

"Who cares about the seasons?" She scowls. "All I do is make cheesecake for Adrian and go shopping with your mother. Thank God for Netflix."

"Here, here," I say.

"I hope you didn't mess up the cheesecakes." Nana looks at the back seat as I park the car in the closest spot to the back door.

"I'm sure they're fine. I'll help you inside and have Donovan get them. Don't worry."

When we step inside, Donovan is talking to the kitchen staff about the menu and placement of the food. I slip past them and find my uncle to tell him to help me get the cheese-cakes out of the car.

"Where's your sister?"

"I don't know. I'm sure she'll be here."

"She better be. I told Marissa to take the night off."

"You did what?" I balk. "So it'll just be us?"

"All you have to do is put plates in front of people, Jo. It's not that difficult."

"Says the man dressed to the nines who won't be putting plates in front of people." I shoot him a look as we step outside.

Thankfully, my sister is parking the shiny white BMW next

to my rusty gold Celica and the three of us are able to get all of the cheesecakes in one trip.

"Mitch is here alone," Misty whispers when we're both behind the bar, pouring glasses of water for everyone.

"So?"

"So isn't that weird?"

I look over the bar out to the tables and focus on the one Mitch is sitting at. He's sitting beside Jagger, who did bring a date along, that Jessa girl. Maverick is also solo woman-wise, but he brought a friend. The entire room is filled with athletes and coaches though, so I guess they're all friends.

"Well, you always said Mitch's first love was baseball. I guess that hasn't changed."

"You're right. I thought that was just an excuse he made to get rid of me," she says softly.

"I don't think anyone would ever want to get rid of you." I set my hand over hers and squeeze it. "And if they do, they're crazy."

"True." She smiles and looks over at their table again. "Who's the girl Jag's with?"

"Jessa."

"I take it we don't like her?" Misty laughs.

"What makes you say that?"

"The way you just said her name like she's gum stuck to the bottom of your shoe."

"She's the one we walked in on him with."

"Ohhhh." Misty frowns slightly. "I vaguely remember that."

"You were drunk." I laugh. "Anyway, they hook up a lot."

"You walked in on them again?"

"No. God no. I just know."

"Hm."

"Whatever." I shrug. "Not my problem."

"But you care." She shoots me a look. "I can tell you care."

"I don't care. Why would I care?"

"Maybe you like him. I mean, he's pretty irresistible and to be living with him? You're bound to develop some kind of feelings for him."

"Besides annoyance?"

"You keep telling yourself that, Jo." Misty laughs as she lifts the tray with waters.

I do the same with the tray beside it and ignore her comment because I truly don't care and I have absolutely no feelings for him. We split up and place waters in front of everyone at the tables. When I get to the table where Jagger is sitting, I make it a point to avoid all eye contact, which is hard. He's wearing a black suit and has brushed his hair to the side and looks so fucking hot. I hate myself for thinking it.

"Hey, you're Lawrence Fisher's girlfriend," one guy says.

"Ex-girlfriend," Jagger answers for me. I shoot him a look that says mind your business.

"Shit, you guys broke up?" The guy raises an eyebrow. "He's about to get paid."

"He's a piece of shit," Jagger says. "Fuck him and his millions."

The guy starts cackling. I walk away quickly.

"What was that about?" Misty asks when we're back behind the bar.

"Nothing." I keep my gaze on Jagger's profile wishing he'd look at me so I can flip him off. He doesn't look. Jessa sets a hand on his shoulder though and I find myself silently seething.

"Girls. Pick up the pace. The salads should be out there by now," Uncle Adrian says.

My sister and I go to the kitchen and start setting salad plates on the trays and walk out one behind the other. This time, we both start on the same side of the restaurant. There are only seven tables occupied and the salad plates are pretty small. Uncle Adrian has two guys from the kitchen setting the bread down on each table as we do this. When we reach the Cruz brothers' table, Misty and I freeze momentarily and look at each other. It's an unspoken understanding. She doesn't want to serve Mitch and even though I haven't explained the full situation of Jagger and me, Misty knows I don't want to be near him either. We switch places and I take Mitch's side while she takes the other. I lower my empty tray and start heading to the back when a hand closes around my forearm and stops me. My skin prickles. I don't have to turn around to know it's him, but when I do turn around slowly and find myself staring into his toffee-colored eyes, my pulse starts zapping inside me like I'm being electrocuted.

"Do you need something?"

He lets go of my arm and smiles lazily. "I just wanted to remind you about our agreement."

"What agreement?" My eyes bounce from him to Jessa beside him, who's doing a good job at pretending not to pay attention, and back to him.

"Cheesecake."

"Oh." I let out an awkward laugh. "Sure. Yeah, I totally got you."

The edge of his mouth lifts as he watches me walk away. It takes me the entirety of my walk to calm down. That's fifteen whole steps. There's a reason I don't tell my sister about my reactions to him. For starters, I never told her we hooked up. I tell my sister mostly everything, but I didn't tell her that. Secondly, she'd laugh at me and I wouldn't blame her. I mean, how could I have this response to a man I live with but am not with? It's ridiculous.

"Main courses are next. Then cheesecake," Uncle Adrian says. "Why don't the two of you sit down and let these guys serve the main courses and cheesecake?"

"We're here to work," Misty says.

"I'm still paying you. Don't worry." Uncle Adrian chuckles. "But Donovan had two extras come in tonight that I wasn't expecting so you might as well sit down. Your dad's paying for all of this anyway."

"Okay." Misty looks at me warily. I shrug and start taking my apron off. She does the same. "Should we sit with Mom and Dad?"

"Um, no. That's the boring table. Besides, it's filled up." I look around. "There are two seats available at that one."

"I don't know any of those guys."

"Neither do I, but food is food, and they're kind of cute."

"I thought you said no more college athletes." She tucks her hand into my elbow as we walk over.

"Maybe I changed my mind. Maybe I meant no athletes for boyfriends. I can hook up with one."

"You've never just hooked up with anyone." She laughs. "You're too much of a relationship type."

"You're only saying that because I've been in a relationship for the majority of my college life." I frown.

"Precisely."

"You hook up with guys."

"And I am one hundred percent okay with doing the one-and-done thing."

"I feel like that's what I need in my life right now."

"I agree." She smiles at me with a wink as we reach the table. "And they are kind of cute."

Chapter Seventeen

Jagger

Jo's laugh keeps pulling me out of the conversation my brothers are having. I glance over there for what seems like the hundredth time since she sat at the table next to ours. She's talking to Bobby Yelich from the baseball team and I'd bet money that whatever is coming out of his mouth is not as funny as she's making it out to be.

"Dude, you're staring," Mav whispers in my ear. "And Jessa's right beside you."

"So?"

"So, she's fucking hot and you're staring at Jo."

"So?" I meet his gaze.

"Jessa's a sure bet. Jo? In your dreams." He chuckles. I glare. He laughs harder.

"Fuck you, Mav."

Jessa and I are not a thing. We're not dating. Sure, we hook up, but we have an understanding. She likes being seen with me and I like staying single and keeping my options open. Jessa's a cool girl, anyone would be lucky to have her, but she's ultimately not my type. We like to fuck though and right now that's the most important thing we have in common. I look at Josephine again. She has her hand on Bobby's now and is leaning in as he types something on his phone. Jesus Christ, I hope she didn't give him her phone number. I shake my head. She just got out of one bad relationship and she's going to what, jump into another one? Everyone knows Bobby is one of the biggest players. He's never seen with the same girl twice. I look at Mitch, who's glaring at the other table as well. When I look again, I notice Misty is also sitting there flirting with someone, and shit, these guys are Mitch's teammates. Not that they know he had something with Misty. It was so damn long ago, I even forget sometimes. Obviously, my brother doesn't share that sentiment. Before I know it, he's getting up and going over there. I watch as he interrupts Misty's conversation and she stands up, the two of them walking off to the corner of the room.

"Shit is getting good," Mav says, stuffing another piece of bread into his mouth. I swear he ate the entire loaf and somehow he's still at it. "They're arguing."

"I see that."

"Why are they arguing?" Jessa asks, pressing a hand on my thigh as she scoots a little closer.

"They used to date," Mav says.

"What?" Jessa looks over at them again. "She's really pretty."

"She's gorgeous," Mav says. "She's a Canó. Those two are

like up there with angels. Maybe Victoria's Secret Angels, but angels nonetheless. Definite tens."

Jessa laughs. "What am I then?"

"You're pretty." Mav shrugs a shoulder like he didn't just burn this girl. I stifle a laugh. Sometimes I forget what a savage my brother can be and how much I enjoy it, not that I would enjoy him hurting Jessa, but still.

"What do you think, Jag?" Jessa looks at me. "Am I up there with them?"

"I wasn't the one who said they're up there with any kind of angels and I definitely do not rate women on a number scale." I raise an eyebrow.

She's got me fucked up if she thinks I'm going to enter this conversation. I've seen too many men meet their downfall by giving women the wrong answer and that's just not going to be me. Not tonight anyway. Apparently, my answer is still the wrong answer because Jessa scowls at me, takes her hand off my lap to cross her arms, and faces forward.

"You're rooming with one of them," she says, still not looking at me.

"And?"

"And you think she's hot."

"I never said that."

"She's hot. I'm saying she's hot." Jessa throws daggers at me with her eyes when she looks at me again. "So I know you think she is."

"You're putting words in my mouth." I pick up the Jameson on the rocks I'm having and drink.

"I thought you two were just having fun," Mav says, because Mav can't mind his own fucking business. "I didn't realize it was serious."

"It's not serious," I say.

"It can be if you let it be," Jessa retorts.

I don't know what face I make, but I know I make one because she shakes her head, throws her napkin on the table, and storms off in the direction of the bathroom. I watch her bubbly ass until she disappears down the hall since it'll probably be the last time I ever see it.

"You going to go after her?"

"No."

"You serious?" Mav raises an eyebrow when I meet his eyes.

"You wanna go after her?"

"I can't go after her. You already fucked her."

"So?" Now I feel myself make a face. "You just said we weren't serious."

"Yeah, but that's weird. Would you fuck your friend's ex?" he asks, and I know he's talking about Jo.

Maybe he's not. My brother can be so dense sometimes. Either way, I ignore his statement. The fact of the matter is, Lawrence crossed the line first and technically I had Jo first. Lawrence knew I liked her and he went after her anyway, probably as a way to get back at me for not going to Duke and becoming one of his receivers. Well, fuck Lawrence and fuck Duke and fuck Bobby Yelich. I take another sip of my drink before setting it down. Josephine laughs again; this time her throaty laugh makes my heartbeat catch.

"Man, I didn't know Bobby was that funny," Mav says.

"He's not."

"You know him?"

"No."

Mav chuckles. "You jealous?"

"Hell no." I scowl.

"Sure looks like it."

My phone vibrates in my pocket and I pull it out to see a text from Jessa.

Jessa: I'm leaving. I already got an Uber.

Me: I can take you.

Jessa: I don't want you to.

Me: I don't mind.

Jessa: What is this? What we're doing? I thought maybe we were going somewhere.

Me: I told you I didn't want a girlfriend. You said you didn't want a boyfriend. I thought we had an agreement.

Jessa: We did.

Me: So?

Jessa: I like you. Things changed.

Me: Not for me.

She sends a sad face emoji and I put my phone away looking up just in time to see Mitch walking back to the table and Misty disappearing through the back door. Jo notices and gets up to go after her sister. Bobby and the other guy keep talking and dabbing like they won some kind of prize, but I focus on Mitch when he sits down. He looks over at me.

"Where's Jessa?"

"She left."

"Okay?" He frowns. "Alone?"

"She called an Uber."

"Why?"

"What were you and Misty talking about?" I ask.

"Life. Just catching up."

"Hm." I take another sip of my drink. "Is that why she left looking pissed off?"

"Misty is her own person. I don't decide how she reacts to the things we talk about."

I laugh. "Okay, you fucking weirdo."

"I asked her to come visit me in New York," he says after a long, silent moment.

I blink. Mav blinks. The rest of the table is silent. The rest of the table are three guys from Mitch's baseball team as well. It's not like they're untrustworthy or whatever but my brother isn't much of a sharer so it surprises me that he said that aloud without a second thought.

"I take it she turned you down?" Yamil says across the table.

"Yep." Mitch sighs heavily. "She says my first love will always be baseball and she'd always come second and she doesn't think she can handle it and that if I do get signed she can't bear to endure another heartbreak."

"Did you tell her that wasn't true and that baseball won't always come first?" Mav asks.

"Why would I lie to her?" Mitch lets out a forced laugh. "She's not wrong."

"You two are going to die alone," Mav says, shaking his

head. "You're so focused on yourselves that you forget you need other people."

"Says the guy who spends more than half his time playing video games."

"Hey, I'm getting paid to test out video games." He shrugs a shoulder. "I'm okay with that."

"For now. Wait till hockey season starts and you're wrapped up in that," Mitch says.

When the food arrives and it's not Misty or Jo serving it, I start to wonder if they left. In the time between the food and the cheesecake, Henry comes over and starts talking to us with some friends, and I have to push Jo out of my mind, but not completely. Is she still outside? Is she coming back? Does she remember she promised to save me a slice of cake? It doesn't matter. I'm getting cheesecake either way, but I want it to come from her. Even as I think this, I know it's stupid, but it doesn't make a difference. I've made up my mind. I'm going to have my cake and eat it too. Fuck the consequences.

Chapter Eighteen

Jo

"**I** DON'T WANT ANY MORE." I HAND THE JOINT BACK TO MY SISTER and exhale. "My head feels light and I need to be able to have a conversation with Mom and Dad." My own words make me push off the wall, wide-eyed. "Do you think they'll know I'm high?"

"You cannot possibly be high, Jo. You took half a hit of this." She looks at me. "This is medicinal."

"Yeah, for your anxiety, not for mine."

"You don't have anxiety." My sister presses the tip of the joint to her lips and inhales.

"My anxieties lie completely on our parents right now. First I was arrested and then this? They'll kill me." I start pacing. "Dammit."

"Here. Put some Visine in your eyes. It'll be fine. This is supposed to help you relax, not panic."

"I'm not panicking but this absolutely does not help me relax."

"You've only done it twice." Misty laughs.

"Yeah. And look at what happened the first time."

"You walked in on your roommate screwing someone else." She shrugs a shoulder, exhaling. "That's what happens when you move in with a hot guy."

"Misty, this is not funny. I'm seriously freaking out right now." I swear my heart is racing extra fast. Is that normal? I pull out my phone and Google it. "Apparently it's normal."

"What's normal?"

"Dude, are you not listening to me?"

"Jo, you've been quiet for the last five minutes." She eyes me curiously. "Maybe you shouldn't talk to Mom and Dad after all."

"That's what I'm trying to tell you." I put my phone in my back pocket. I look at my car, then at the back door, then take the bottle of Visine she's handing me and apply a drop in each eye. I blink and blink until I think maybe I'm less high. Jesus. I only took one hit of that thing. Never again.

"I'm going back inside," Misty says.

"What?" I gape at her. "I can't go back inside yet."

"So, wait for me out here. I'm getting hungry and we missed dinner by now. I'll go grab us some plates and stuff."

"Okay." I breathe in and out. "I'll wait here."

When Misty goes inside, I start pacing again and focusing on breathing deeply. That has to help, right? Yes. Deep breaths. I keep pacing. The door opens quickly, or at least I think quickly, and I turn around ready to say so until I see Jagger. I take an ex-aggerated step back, even I know I'm being weird, but he looks good, like really good, in black slacks, a white button-down, and a black tie. He left his jacket inside, but his normally wild dark hair is brushed perfectly to the side and his face is shaved and smooth.

"You look really good," I blurt out. The response I get, his lip pulling up slightly and his eyes dancing, makes my heart leap.

"Thank you, Josephine. I think that's the first nice thing you've said to me in years." He raises an eyebrow and shoves his hands in his pockets as he reaches me. "Why are you out here all alone?"

"Um . . . I was with Misty. She's getting food."

"To bring outside?" he asks in a slow voice that makes me wonder how dumb of an idea it was after all. It seemed like a perfectly normal thing to do just minutes ago.

"Yes?"

"You don't sound so sure." His eyes are still dancing. My heart is still hammering.

"I'm high."

"What?" He chuckles. "Right now?"

"Yes." I nod. "I can't go back in there. My parents and Bobby . . ." My eyes widen. "Oh my God. Bobby. I forgot about him."

"Who cares about him?"

"Is he still inside?"

"Yes."

"He's probably waiting for me to give him my number."

"Why would you want to give him your number?" Jagger scowls.

"Because he's cute."

"I thought you were done dating athletes?"

"I am." I blink. "I told you that?"

"You did."

"Hm." I purse my lips. "I'm really thirsty."

"What?" He barks out a laugh, it's a low laugh and it's short-lived but oh my God it sounds so nice.

"I'm parched." I put a hand on my throat.

"Give me a moment." He shakes his head with a sigh, walks back to the door, and disappears inside. Unlike Misty, he's back outside in a second with a bottle of water. He hands it over. I take it, uncap it, and down half of it in light speed.

"Thanks so much." I breathe out when I cap it and lower it. "Water is so good."

"It is."

"It's so sad that so many people don't have access to it. Did you know that?" I feel myself frown. "I mean here in the United States people don't have access to clean water. That's insane."

"It's very sad," he agrees.

"And then you have major assholes like Lawrence who are about to become millionaires and will never do anything about it." I cross my arms.

"What does . . . " He shakes his head and looks away. "So, you and Bobby."

"He's nice, right?"

"I guess."

"You guess?"

"What happened to the no-athlete rule?" He meets my gaze again.

"Misty says I need to have casual relationships for a while, so I figure, if it's going to be casual anyway, who cares?" I shrug. "Kind of like what you and that girl have going on."

"You mean Jessa?"

"Yep." Now it's me who looks away. "You brought her as your date though so maybe it's more than casual."

"It's not."

"Not yet."

"It never will be."

"How do you know?" I look at him again. "Things change and sometimes it does become more."

"In order for it to become more, both people would have to want that, which is not the case with Jessa."

"It is for her."

"How would you know?"

"I saw her crying. She left in an Uber. It doesn't take a rocket scientist to know something happened." I search his eyes.

"We hooked up once." He moves closer. My pulse leaps.

"Once," I whisper.

"That worked out fine."

"Did it?"

"It seemed to. You got what you wanted out of it, didn't you? You moved on rather quickly, too."

"He was very persistent." I swallow. "You weren't."

"What would have happened if I had been?"

"I don't know." It's a total lie. I one thousand percent would have dated him, but he never chased, never showed interest. It was a one and done for him.

"Did you want me to chase you? Were you waiting for me to?" He takes another step forward, completely engulfing the distance between us.

"I don't know," I whisper. "I guess a part of me wanted you to, but I knew deep down that you weren't the chasing type. It doesn't matter anyway."

"Why doesn't it matter?

"You would have broken me."

"I would never hurt you. That's why I never chased. I regretted it though. I regretted it more when you moved on with him." He searches my eyes. "You've been tearing me up inside for years."

"I didn't know you felt anything." I can barely breathe, but somehow I speak the words.

"Of course you didn't." He scoffs.

"What's that supposed to mean?"

"You haven't even been around. You've spent so much of your time at Duke freaking parties." He makes a face as he says the words, as if merely speaking it aloud leaves a taste in his mouth. "How would you know? You dropped classes I was in. You walked away from parties we both attended—"

"Because even though we both know you're not the chasing type and you're definitely not the settling down type, you kept coming on to me at those parties!"

"Because I wanted you." He takes one last step forward

with the force of his words and closes the remaining distance between us. My heart leaps into my throat as I stare into his thunderous gaze. He looks like he's looking for a fight, or worse, like he might devour me right here. He takes a breath and lowers his voice, and the timbre does absolutely nothing to calm my emotions. "I've wanted you since we were teenagers. I wanted you at that party and after I had you, I knew it would never be enough." His words are a low growl, a harsh whisper against my lips. "I've wanted you every day since and seeing you with him was like eating glass. Is that what you want to hear? Is that what it'll take for you to finally pick me?"

"You're an idiot, Jagger Cruz. I would have picked you from day one and you know it."

"Day one doesn't count."

"Day one meant everything to me." I lift a hand and run it up his torso, setting it on his shoulder. "You were my first, you know."

"I remember." His gaze darkens. I swear I feel him shaking beneath my hand. "Fuck, Josephine. Just . . . "

I stand on the tips of my toes and move my hand so that it's on the back of his neck and kiss him. In my mind, I'm in control of this kiss, but when he moves into it and his large hands finally touch me, I feel myself unravel and when he backs me into the wall behind me and presses into me, his mouth devouring mine, I know I'm not in control of anything at all. I realize that this is what I crave and am afraid of. Memories of our hookup flood back to me and I know that underneath all of the lust there's a genuine fear of what would happen if things don't work out. We weren't just friends. Our parents are friends, almost like family in the sense that when shit goes sideways they always count on each other to be there. A relationship between us would carry the weight of the responsibility that if we didn't work out, we'd still see each other and be expected to act cordial. With a shuddering breath, I pull away from the kiss, drunk from it, and look into his eyes. He looks wild, barely contained, his breathing heavy as if he'd been on the field.

"You think too much," he says finally.

"You don't think enough."

"That's why I have more fun." His lip twists into a smirk. "You said you wanted casual. Do casual with me."

My heart thunders. I want to say I don't think I can. I want to say no way, I could never. I want to guard myself from the heartache I know will come from it. Instead, I nod and accept because if I'm going to do casual anyway, it might as well be with the hottest guy I've ever known.

Chapter Nineteen

Jagger

Y OU WOULD THINK AFTER THAT KISS I'D TAKE HER HOME AND FUCK her brains out. You'd be wrong. Somehow, we went from being interrupted by Misty, who brought out a tray of food that Josephine turned down since she was no longer hungry and that turned into me having to drive Misty, who was a little tipsy, and their grandmother Sabrina home, and of course, Jo, who was going to get an Uber because she'd smoked some weed with Misty and unlike Misty, Jo was seemingly terrified of driving under any influence even if she was absolutely sober by the time all of us left the restaurant.

"Your car smells new. Is it new?" her grandmother asks. She's sitting in the passenger seat and has not stopped touching things, from the air vents to the radio.

"It's not, but I've rarely driven it. It stays here when we go back to New York for breaks."

"This is the car you should get, Josephine," she announces.

I glance up in the rearview and find Jo's hazel eyes on mine. My heart instantly kicks into high gear. God, I want her. I want her so badly I can barely stand it. She must see it in my eyes because it takes her a long moment to clear her throat and answer her grandmother.

"Sure, Nana, I'll get right on it. Are you going to write the generous check or will I have to wait for my inheritance to kick in?" Jo asks. I find myself fighting a smile.

"I'll help you buy a car," Misty announces. "Maybe not this one, but a nicer one."

"Why are you grounded, Josephine? You never told me," her grandmother says.

"I made a mistake."

"What kind of mistake?"

"The kind that gets you kicked off the volleyball team." Jo's no longer looking at me, but down at her lap and dammit, I hate it. I want her eyes on mine.

"You got kicked off the volleyball team?" Her grandmother turns slightly in the passenger seat with a gasp. "But you were the best one on the team."

"I wasn't the best one." Jo lets out a short laugh.

"Nonsense. I saw you play."

"Nana, how's your Netflix show binging coming along?" Misty asks randomly. "Are you still watching *Casa de Papel*?"

"Yes but they changed the title and it took me two weeks to realize it. It is now called *Money Heist*." Her grandmother doesn't sound pleased by this. "So I'm a little behind."

"That's a good one though," Misty says. "You have to give me recommendations. I haven't been watching anything since I'm so busy with school."

"Are you still going to graduate early?"

"I am." I can hear the pride in Misty's voice and it makes me smile.

"She's going to graduate and get a bad ass job in New York," Josephine adds. It makes me smile wider. The Canó sisters have always been thick as thieves, much like my brothers and me, and it's something we've always silently respected about one another.

"Misty, let me know what building it is." I turn onto the street she plugged into my GPS.

"You forgot your way around here?" Misty asks with a tsk. "The Cruz brothers move to New York and forget their country roots."

"We moved when I was thirteen," I remind her. "And I normally don't drive on enemy territory if I can help it."

"Enemy territory." Misty laughs. "You can stop up ahead to the right."

I do as instructed and wait for her to gather her jacket and purse and the bag of leftovers we were each given to take home. Once she does that, she kisses Jo on the cheek and makes her promise to text her when she gets home, taps me on the shoulder and thanks me, and walks over to the passenger side window to kiss her grandmother good night. We wait until she's inside the building and waving at us before I drive away.

"Your turn, Nana." I glance over at her with a smile.

"So, tell me, Jagger, how is New York these days?"

"It's . . . New York. Always hectic, always exciting."

"So you don't see yourself staying here after graduation?"

"Probably not."

"He's a city boy through and through, Nana," Jo says from the back seat with a yawn. "Besides, he may go to the NFL and if he does he'll have to go to whatever city gives him a better contract."

"Are we boring you, Josephine?" Nana asks.

"No, ma'am. I can't think about anything more exciting to talk about than Jagger's plans for the future." She yawns again. I shake my head, fighting a smile.

"What are your plans for the future?" I meet her gaze in the rearview.

"I'm just trying to survive this semester." She glances down at her hands again. "I had all these elaborate plans, but after the summer I had, I just want to focus on one day at a time."

"That's fair."

"Smart," Nana says. "But I still haven't heard what exactly happened this summer. I can't believe they kicked you off the volleyball team!"

"I'm surprised you still live all the way out here," I say, trying to change the subject, for Jo's sake even though I'm dying to hear details about her summer.

"When Henry decided to move here and Ray and I followed, there was nothing out here. I liked that. It reminded me of my farm back home, but now, now look at this place," she says as I pull into her driveway.

"You have everything right in front of you." I nod, looking at the plaza across the street. There's everything from a grocery store to a popular makeup chain.

"It's preposterous, if you ask me. Ray would be annoyed by all of the traffic if he was still here. And our new neighbors, don't even get me started on them. They complained about my chickens, as if we don't have enough land between us." Nana starts getting out of the car, but Josephine beats her to the door and I scramble to get out so I can walk her up the few steps, not that Nana needs my help. She's a grandmother, sure, but I'd bet money she's as agile as a twenty-year-old. She says good night to Jo before walking up the steps and I follow. "Thank you for the ride," she says after unlocking her door. "Next time I need to go somewhere, I'm calling you so you can pick me up. Josephine's car is entirely too uncomfortable."

"I'll be here." I wink and jog back down the steps.

Josephine's sitting in the passenger seat now, reaching over and messing with the radio. For a second I wonder if our moment is over, if the kiss was just a fleeting lapse of judgment, but when our eyes meet through the windshield I feel a spark and I know moments with Jo, if not taken for granted, could never be fleeting.

Chapter Twenty

MY PHONE BUZZES ON MY LAP AND I SEE A TEXT FROM BOBBY that says, *It was nice to meet you. Let's go out soon.* Misty dutifully gave him my number when she ran back inside to get my food. I smile at the text because guys don't normally text the same night. Or do they? I don't even know anymore. After Lawrence, I haven't dated anyone, and Lawrence and I started on Instagram, so it's not like he texted right away either. I look at Jagger, who's focused on driving.

"Do guys usually text the same night they meet someone?"

"Bobby texted?" He slides his eyes over to me and back to the road. "I thought we agreed you'd use my body."

"*Use* your body?" I laugh.

"That's what a casual hookup is." He shrugs a shoulder.

Is it? I wouldn't know. I glance out the window and focus on the trees and houses and strip malls. The kiss we shared is still tingling my lips. The thought of more is causing a burning deep in my stomach. I'm living with him though. How will that work? Will we hook up in the living room and then sleep in our respective rooms? Uneasiness starts to take over the previous burning feeling.

"I think we need rules," I blurt out.

"Rules?" He parallel parks in front of our shared house.

"Yes. Rules. Like are we going to hook up and then go to our separate bedrooms?"

"What do you want to do?"

"I think it's best we stay in separate rooms." I lick my lips. "Just in case."

"Just in case?" His mouth twitches but he doesn't push. "Okay. What else?"

"Will we still be allowed to date other people?" I unbuckle my seat belt, but instead of getting out of the car, turn to face him in my seat. He does the same.

"I don't date." He says it with a look on his face that almost looks bewildered by the mere idea of dating and makes me believe him.

"You don't take the women you hook up with to dinner?"

"Not if I can help it."

"Why?" This makes me laugh for some reason, the ridiculous fact that he sticks his dick in someone's vagina but won't share a meal with her.

"I don't know. They want to fuck a football star. They don't care about dinner."

"You've asked?"

"I don't have to ask, Jo. It's pretty obvious when someone grabs your dick in public that they're not thinking about food."

"Hm." That gives me pause, but it makes sense.

When I was dating Lawrence, women never stopped flirting with him and I thought maybe they wanted to date him but that obviously wasn't the case. He cheated on me more times than I realized and he still wasn't dating any of them.

"I thought you wanted casual," Jagger says after a moment. "Dating isn't casual."

"Just because I go on a date with someone doesn't mean I'll sleep with them. I just want to set ground rules so that this doesn't become a problem if I decide to go grab coffee with another guy."

"You can grab coffee with whomever you like."

"Okay then. What about sleeping around?"

"What about it?" He raises an eyebrow.

"Will you still hook up with other women?"

"Do you want me to?"

"I'm not sure." I bite my lip. I'm really not. I don't consider myself a jealous person, but the times I've seen Jagger with other women I have definitely felt something. "Maybe we should revisit this one."

"Okay." He searches my eyes. "Are we done talking?"

My pulse leaps. "I think so."

"Good." He switches the car off and walks outside.

I grab the bag of leftovers at my feet and set a hand on the door, but he's already opening it for me. When I step out of the car, he grabs the bags from my hand and pushes the car door shut. We walk into the house in silence, anticipation growing with each step. I really haven't done this in a long time and I don't know how to start. Normally, with Lawrence, we'd both be in bed getting ready to go to sleep and it would start gradually. With Jagger it seems foreign, like I'm completely starting over and don't know what to do. He tosses his keys on the entrance table, sets the bags of food on the table, and looks over at me.

"You seem nervous."

"I am."

"Are you nervous because it's me or . . . " He starts walking toward me.

"I don't know." My heart is pounding so hard, my chest hurts. I'm one thousand percent nervous because it's him. I try to envision this moment with someone like Bobby and I know I wouldn't be reacting this way.

"This doesn't even feel real." He lifts a hand up and cups my face, his thumb brushing along my bottom lip. My mouth parts with an inhale. "I'm half expecting someone to show up and end this before it even starts."

"Maybe we should," I whisper. "Maybe that's your conscience telling you this shouldn't happen."

"What is yours saying?" His eyes darken with the question.

"I can't hear it. My heart is roaring too loudly and drowning it out."

"Aren't you supposed to follow your heart?"

"I don't know." I gasp when his hand moves and tightens on the nape of my neck, pulling me forward until our lips almost meet, but not quite.

"You need to decide," he whispers against me. "I don't want you to regret this in the morning." He pulls away slightly to search my eyes as if he knows that's what I'm worried about and he's looking for some sort of confirmation. I decide that I won't allow myself to regret this. I want him too much. I need him right now.

"I want you," I say, finally, and he crashes his lips to mine, growling as he deepens the kiss, his fingers wrapping into the hair at the nape of my neck and pulling as he walks me backwards.

My knees hit the couch and we both come crashing down on it. He lets go of me just in time to catch himself from completely landing on me and pulls away from the kiss. Hooded eyes look down on me and my chest suddenly feels full, a heaviness of inexplicable emotions ricocheting. Instead of giving them attention, I focus on unbuttoning his dress shirt, my hands shaking with nerves, with desire, with the absolute need for this. He brings a hand to my face, his long fingers running along the side of my neck, his thumb on my chin, brushing over my lower lip as I reach the last button. I tear my gaze from his and look at his torso, tanned and toned, every single muscle cut and defined as if he were etched. He lifts up and finishes taking the shirt off, tossing it on the floor. Instead of coming right back down, he stays sitting back on his heel and stands up.

"I'll be right back." He leans down and kisses me in a way that renders me speechless and leaves me writhing even as he pulls away. "Don't move."

He rushes off, I assume to get a condom. I sit up, take my

shirt off, shimmy my jeans down and stay in the black bra and black boy shorts I'm wearing. When he jogs back, he stops short by the armrest, his toffee-colored eyes blazing like fire as they rake over me slowly. He licks his lips, a move that shoots straight between my legs, and tosses the condom on the table beside us as he closes the distance between us.

"Damn," he says, a hoarse whisper followed by a swallow.

He begins taking his pants off, unbuckling the designer belt before working on the button and zipper. There's a large bulk that's impossible to miss and takes my breath away just a little at the memory of what's hiding underneath. Maybe it's because he was my first, but I've never forgotten how beautiful and perfect his cock is. Granted, I only have a couple of others to compare it to—the guy from high school I jerked off in the back row of the movie theatre and Lawrence. Neither compare to Jagger's. That's a terrible thing when he's not only just my rebound but also someone who only does casual. He finishes undressing and soon he's completely naked in front of me and I feel wetter than ever as I take in his physique. I decide casual dick shouldn't be this magnificent. It's unfair, really, but at least I know it's casual going into it. When he meets me on the couch again, his lips are soft against mine, but still hungry, his calloused fingertips grazing over my bare shoulder and down my arm, the other snaking underneath my bra strap and then to my back where he expertly snaps it off with two fingers, a move that speaks volumes. He did it the first time, the only time, we were together, and even then it gave me pause but I find that the only thing I want to do is give in to him and there isn't much he can do or say to stop that from being the case.

His lips leave mine and his gaze flickers to mine as he drags the straps of my bra down my arms slowly, not looking away even after he tosses the bra aside. His hand caresses the side of my face, and it feels so intimate that I have to fight the urge to pull away and plead with him to just fuck me and not take his time with me. A part of me wants to. A part of me knows that this is why he leaves a trace of casualties behind. He takes his time. He makes you feel like you're the only one, the most important one, and maybe I am right now, for a moment. I decide to get lost in that reality, and it's the way he kisses me and touches me ever so gently, with that fire in his eyes, that makes me stop overthinking this. He brings a hand between my legs and tucks it into my underwear, groaning when his fingers slide against my slickness.

"You're so ready for me." He presses his lips against mine, moving so that he's off the couch and slipping my underwear off with one hand as he continues to play with my pussy with the other.

His mouth leaves mine and explores my body, my neck, my chest, my nipples as his fingers dive inside of me with such force my entire body bends off the couch in a gasp. His thumb presses down on my clit as his fingers go deeper and I find that the only thing I can do is grind against his hand, my eyes rolling to the back of my head as the first sensation of the orgasm washes over me. His mouth is still locked on my nipple when he slides his fingers out of me and wipes his hand, slick with my desire, over my thigh. I think I make a sound, a pout, saying I don't want him to stop, but that's before I hear the condom wrapper and my eyes pop open to see him sliding it on. He leans over me, one arm over my head, holding on to the couch, the other hand guiding his cock between my legs.

"I want to take my time with you," he says, pausing to bite his lip as the tip teases my clit. "But I can't right now. I've waited so long, Josephine."

He begins thrusting inside of me, inch by inch, his stroke slow as he fills me, and once he's completely in he stops moving, the hand he'd used to guide himself into me now gripping my waist, his eyes shut as he breathes through his nose roughly.

"Fuck, you're tight." He bites his bottom lip, eyes still closed, and I feel my chest constrict.

The need for him to move is too great, and even though I know he's savoring this, having him inside me, filling me like this, and not having him move is absolute torture, so I swing my hips once, earning a groan from him, twice, making his eyes pop open and find mine, three times, making his grip tighten more so, but it's that third time that makes him move, really move. He fucks me hard, my head hitting the top of the couch with each thrust. He presses against me until he hits my pelvic bone and slides out in such a way that I find I cannot breathe. He brings his hand between us and starts playing with my clit as he slams into me. I try and fail not to make embarrassing sounds, but I feel myself shatter beneath him just as my words get louder, and it's the scream that rips out of me that makes him come undone.

The aftermath is awkward, for me, at least. Jagger pulls out of me slowly and I wince, feeling every bit of his absence. He helps me get on my feet and once I'm up, I pick up my things and idle for a second. Thankfully, he walks to the bathroom and I disappear into my bedroom and wait until I hear him finish with the bathroom before I go in there. While I'm washing my hair, I try to figure out everything I should say to him when I see him, but come up blank. I don't know what it is about him that makes me think I can't do casual with him. Maybe it's because he was my first and they say you never forget your first. Maybe I actually like him more than I want to admit. My answer comes when I walk out of the bathroom and Jagger's nowhere to be found. This is good. I don't have to say anything at all. This is what I want. I just didn't expect it to make me feel this empty.

Chapter Twenty-One

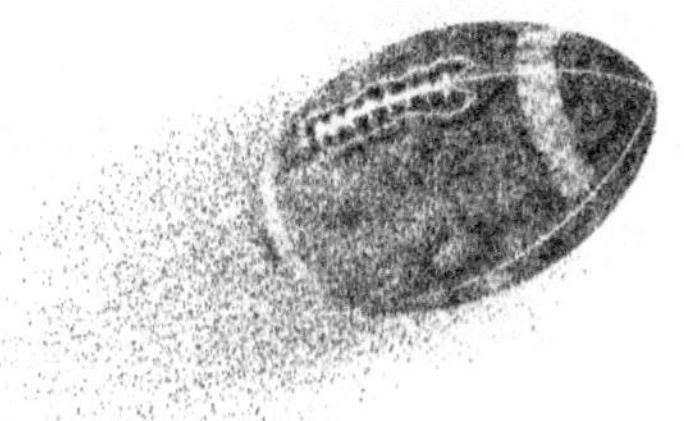

Jo

I COULDN'T SLEEP. I GOT UP AT FIVE AND NOTICED JAGGER'S DOOR was ajar and he wasn't in the house, and that made me go down a rabbit hole of what-ifs, one I'm all too familiar with, since it's the same what-ifs that haunted me throughout the majority of my relationship with Lawrence. What if I did something wrong? What if he decided what we did was a stupid mistake? What if he regrets me? I left as soon as I could, taking an Uber to the restaurant to pick up my car and gathering my thoughts on the way to math class. Now I'm sitting here, chewing off my cuticles, wondering if I should've come today. Needless to say, no thoughts were gathered on the ride over.

I keep replaying last night in my head. The way he looked at me, the way he kissed me, the way he touched me, and I can't stop feeling things I'm not ready to feel. I can't remember feeling this way with Lawrence, although I'm sure I must have in the beginning, but that was before everything that happened to spoil what once was and in truth I can barely remember how things were before they turned tumultuous. The class started filling in and I spot Jessa talking to a friend as they take their seats in the middle of the room. I wonder if things will be awkward or if she'll just ignore Jagger altogether. *Why do I care?* I don't know, but I do.

Jagger walks into the room just seconds later and my heart launches into my throat. He's wearing a black T-shirt and jeans and his hair is slicked back, obviously wet from a shower. I bite my lip just thinking about what's underneath all of those clothes. I bite it harder when he turns those eyes in my direction and holds my gaze. He doesn't smile, doesn't do anything at all that screams we had sex last night, and yet, as he walks over to me and takes a seat in the empty chair beside me, I feel like everyone knows.

"You left early." He stretches his long legs and leans back in his chair, turning his face to me.

"I left early?" I raise an eyebrow. "You left earlier."

"I went for a run."

"A run? It was still dark out."

"Five. Five miles at five." He says it like it's totally normal to run that many miles at any time of day, but I guess for him it is. I used to run three every day, now I'm down to one if I'm lucky. I swallow.

"I left to pick up my car."

"I would have taken you."

"I know, but I didn't know where you were or whether or

not you were coming back so . . ." I shrug, licking my lips. His eyes go there, so I look away, my face burning with memories.

"You regret last night." His voice is low, but hard, and when I look at him his jaw is tight and his eyes are cloudy and I know he's pissed.

"I didn't say that."

"You don't have to." He faces forward and before I can say anything else, the professor starts speaking.

The entire class, I have a knot in the pit of my stomach and I hate it. I hate that he thinks I regret it. I want to scream that I don't regret it at all, it's just . . . it's a tricky situation and I don't want to develop feelings for him. He's a master at casual hookups and I'm a novice. I just need time to catch up. When class is over, Jagger bolts out of the room like his feet are on fire and I don't get the chance to remedy what happened. My phone buzzes and I see Lawrence's face on the screen. I push the side button to ignore the call and sigh heavily. I still haven't signed the paper.

The bar is a blur. Marissa keeps talking to me about some guy she's dating, a slightly older guy who's in the middle of developing a start-up and may move to California.

"He asked me to go with him," she says as she pours one of the beers on tap for tonight.

"Are you going to?"

"Why the hell not?" She shrugs a shoulder. "I'm waiting tables here. Might as well wait them there."

"I guess that's true." I smile. "It'll be an adventure."

"Well, let's not get ahead of ourselves. He's still working on it. He wouldn't leave till next year and who knows what will happen from now to then."

I think about that the entire car ride to my dad's practice. A year is a long time. This time last year, I was rooming with Kelsey, my first friend here and teammate, and we were arguing over empty cereal bowls. I was with Lawrence the majority of the time and truly thought we had a future together. Of course, that was before I found out he was a lying cheater. If you'd asked me then, even despite my annoyance at him half of the time, I would have still told you I might marry him. I mean, that's what you did, right? You got into long relationships with that end goal in mind? I didn't know anymore and now I knew less. When I get to Dad's, Donna is walking out.

"You're leaving?" I look at the time on my phone. "This early?"

"I am." She smiles. "Your father's in his office. Lock up when you go inside."

"I will." I frown as I walk in and do as instructed, then shut my eyes momentarily before walking over to Dad's office. He's on the phone, so he holds a finger up to me.

"Is he there now?" he asks whoever he's speaking to. "Where's Barnes? Are you fucking kidding me? Yeah." He sighs, glancing at the Rolex Mom gave him for his birthday last year.

"Yeah, I guess I can make it. Prep him." He hangs up and I stop biting my lip.

"Surgery?"

"Yep. It was Barnes's day, but he felt sick, left, and tested positive for the flu."

"Oh, no." I frown. "So you're working late?"

"Unfortunately." He stands with a heavy sigh as he sorts out paperwork. "Jagger should be coming in tonight, but I won't be able to help, so he'll have to come back another night."

"I'll let him know." I nod.

"Do you remember your stretches?" Dad walks around the desk and walks toward me. My eyes widen. He can't possibly be asking me what I think he's asking.

"Dad, no way."

"Just teach him the ones he can do at home. You don't have to stretch his arm for him if you're not comfortable with it, but you've been through it, so if you are comfortable . . . " He tilts his head slightly as he leans in to kiss the top of my head. "I love you, J. See you this weekend. Lock up when you leave."

"Okay," I call out, too shocked to fully comprehend what he's just asked of me.

What I should have done was ask if stretching Jagger's arm will let me off the hook of cleaning the floors, but I just . . . I take a deep breath and go from room to room to see which one I can use. Not that I need a room to teach him a few stretches. I can do that right here in the hall. Still, I can't help the feeling of importance that seeps in as I think about playing physical therapist for the day. I decide room four is the best one. It's small and doesn't have all of the high-tech stuff the other ones have, but it's the room I rehabbed my shoulder in five years ago and it's cozy. I'm walking back to the main area when I hear the knock on the door. My heart picks up speed as I walk over and unlock it, opening it for Jagger. He's wearing black basketball shorts and a baby blue T-shirt with a football on it.

"My dad had to leave," I say, but Jagger is already walking past me and into the practice. I shut the door and lock it, turning to face him. "He's in surgery now so he told me to teach you some stretches or help you stretch your arm. Whatever you're comfortable with."

"Whatever I'm comfortable with?" His eyes are alight with humor when he turns to face me.

"Yeah. I mean I'm okay with it if you are."

He chuckles quietly, shaking his head as he looks at the ground.

"I don't see how that's funny." I start walking to the available room and hear him walking behind me. When we get there, I walk in and shut the door behind us, then think better of it, but leave it shut anyway.

"It's funny," he says, taking his shirt off over his head with a wince. "Because I had my fingers and dick inside of you just last night, so I don't understand why I'd be uncomfortable with this." He raises an eyebrow at me as he tosses his shirt onto the chair across the room. "You on the other hand are full of regret."

"Oh my God." I feel every word pound into me just like he did last night and busy myself with the table he has to lie on, ignoring the way I'm blushing furiously.

Lawrence was never a dirty talker. Not like this. When I'm ready, but still blushing, I turn to face him. It's a mistake. He's not wearing a shirt and seeing his ripped body like that on full display is a reminder of what we did, a reminder that makes my fingers shake because of how badly I want to reach out and scratch every perfect cut as he reams into me. God help me. Jagger starts to close the distance between us, his gaze heating with each step. When he reaches me, he lifts my chin up so that I'm looking at him.

"Tell me you don't regret me." His words are a low growl.

"I don't regret you," I whisper, unsure of why tears are suddenly springing to my eyes.

Maybe because all those years ago when I walked out after we had sex, I had the awful feeling that he would think I regretted him. Maybe because all these years that's the reason I've dodged him, because I couldn't face the fact that I definitely wanted him more than I cared to admit and didn't want to look in his eyes to see whether or not there was hatred there, or worse, pain.

"Tell me what you need, Josephine," he says, bringing his hand from my chin to the nape of my neck.

I tilt my head back and he kisses the exposed curve of my neck, he traces wet kisses up and down slowly. My nipples pebble in my shirt and my hands fly to the waistband of his shorts. He pulls away, desire clouding his eyes, igniting a fire inside me that makes me feel exposed, feral.

"I want you," I manage.

"Hm. How do you want me?" Another growl, this time as

he kisses me, his lips soft, his tongue lashing as hard as the grip he has on my hair.

"Any way. Any way I can have you." I whimper, but I don't want him to stop.

I lean into him, against him, wanting more, begging for more. Anything to douse the fire and sate this ridiculous need for him. With his free hand, he starts undoing the button of my jeans. He's still kissing me as he lowers them and only pulls away to take my shirt off quickly before his lips attack mine again. He takes off my bra quickly and lowers it slowly, reaching for my nipple and tugging it. I moan at that, pushing against him, needing more. He pulls away again and lets go of the hair on the nape of my neck, backing up an inch to study me.

"You're so fucking perfect," he says, like it's a curse, like he's upset.

I huff out a laugh because I could say the same about him. I'm just scared to say anything at all right now, not wanting to break this spell. He dips his head and pulls my breast into his mouth, licking, tugging, making me squirm. He uses one hand to steady himself on the bed behind me and runs the other down my stomach and into my panties. A sound elicits from his lips, the guttural vibration of it against my nipple is almost too much. I grab a fistful of his full, messy hair with one hand and his hand beside me with the other. He lets go of my nipple, a soft *pop* in the otherwise quiet room, and makes his way up to my neck, burying his face there as he begins to stroke my folds with his fingers.

"So wet. So fucking wet," he groans against me. "Get on this thing."

I comply, kicking off my jeans and pulling myself onto the patient bed behind me. The white paper that covers it scrunches beneath my fists and Jagger lowers himself to his knees, pulling my thong to the side as he settles between my legs and licks along the seam of my folds. I grip the paper harder, letting out a huff of a breath.

"So good," he murmurs against me, biting the inside of my thigh before sucking on my clit.

"Oh my . . . don't stop." I buck toward his mouth, letting go of the paper with one hand, and grab a fistful of his hair.

He groans against my clit and brings his hands up to grip my ass, pulling me against his mouth as he moves hungrily, his tongue unyielding. I can barely breathe, my heart quickening more than ever before as the shock of the orgasm hits me. Jagger continues licking, teasing, biting my thighs as I come down from ecstasy. When he stands, he's already pulling down his basketball shorts and briefs, freeing himself between us. I reach out and wrap a hand around him, stroking as he gets closer to me. He hands me the condom wrapper and I take it, letting go of him only to slide it on slowly. With the way his muscles are all tight, I know he's doing everything he can not to pounce.

He reaches behind my neck and pulls my face close to his as I position him at my entrance, and he kisses me deeply as he slides inside of me slowly. He doesn't fuck me fast and hard today, but takes my breath away nonetheless. His thrusts are shallow at first as his tongue dances with mine. His fingers pinch my right nipple and when I moan into his mouth, he begins to move a little faster, a little deeper, his girth stretching me to invite him in fully. My hips tip just slightly, meeting his thrusts, which become harder, but still languid, and I reach around his neck to maintain balance. He pulls away from the kiss tentatively, his dick still sliding in and out of me as he meets my gaze, and it's a lot, too much. I kiss him again so that I don't have to look into his eyes and try to decipher what's there and what's not. So that I don't have to have my heart broken again just yet, not by him, not by anyone. So that I don't have to end this in fear of that, and when I deepen the kiss with a gasp because I'm coming again, he fucks me even harder.

Chapter Twenty-Two

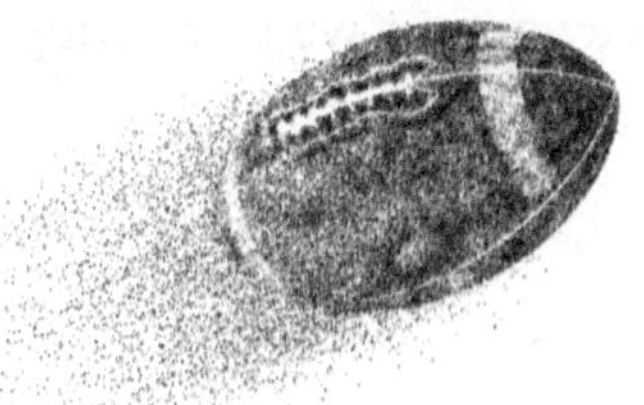

Jo

"WE'RE GOING TO A PARTY TONIGHT."

"Another pre-med frat party?"

"No. A regular frat party." Misty laughs in my ears. I have earphones on while I clean up the bar for the night shift.

"I work until ten."

"That's fine. I'll pick you up at eleven-thirty. Don't worry, we'll Uber."

"Is it a Duke party?"

"Actually, it's on your side of town." She laughs. "Dylan invited me, which means Bobby will be there."

"Which means you're playing with fire because when Mitch finds out he's going to have a cow." I smile as I say the words because my sister doesn't care if Mitch has a cow or a herd, she'll do what she wants just the same.

"Mitch and I are history, Jo. Over. Period. Besides, Dylan and I are super casual. I'm not getting involved with another baseball player."

"True." I bite my lip. I still haven't told her about Jagger and I don't think I'm quite ready to yet. "So where's the party? By my house?"

"Like two blocks away, but we're wearing heels and short dresses so we're not walking."

"What?" I stop wiping the counter. "You picked out my outfit?"

"Dude, yes. I don't want you wearing skinnies and a band T-shirt yet again."

I keep frowning, but I understand what my sister's getting at, so I don't even comment. I don't mind dressing up. I think of Jagger and wonder whether or not I should tell him about the party, maybe invite him? No. I shake my head. This is casual. Inviting him to a party feels like I'm expecting more and I don't want to come off as the girl who falls for the guy just because she had amazing sex with him twice. This is yet another reason I should tell my sister what's happening. I sigh heavily.

"What?" Misty's distracted. "If you want to wear a damn band T-shirt, fine, but you have to at least wear a skirt."

"No." I laugh half-heartedly. "It's not about that. I'll wear a dress. I just . . . I have to tell you something."

"Okay."

"I hooked up with Jagger," I whisper, looking around as if I'm not completely alone at the bar. The kitchen people are here, but they never come out front.

"What?" she asks loudly. "Wait. What? When?"

"It's happened twice." I bite my lip.

"And?"

"And what?"

"How was it?"

"Good. Really good. Better than good." I stand up straight, catching myself before I say anything else that makes me sound like I'm falling for him. "But it's casual. We both agreed."

"Well, yeah, it's casual. Jagger doesn't even date." She laughs, then stops. "Does he?"

"Apparently not."

"Are you feeling okay about it?"

"I am." I nod, even though she can't see me. "Shocking, right?"

"Not shocking. That's what happens when you decide to take matters into your own hands and do what men have been doing for centuries. Have fun with it. Don't get invested."

"I'm doing that."

"So you're allowed to see other people since it's casual and all? Have you spoken about that?"

"Yeah. He says he doesn't care if I date."

"Okay, good because Dylan just texted saying that Bobby's coming with, so it'll be a very casual double date."

"That's fine. I guess." I put the used cloth in the bucket where all the dirty rags go, take out a clean one, and walk toward the door, unlocking it and pulling the cute Sangria sign my aunt drew for it. "I have to go. I'll see you later."

"Be ready by eleven-thirty!"

"I will."

My shift is slow. Normally on weekends it picks up, but for some odd reason there are only five tables here tonight, all drinking beer and watching a Tottenham soccer match. I know this because I had to look for the television channel while they yelled for me to stop when I found it. They're nice though, so there's that. Marissa gets to the bar at nine and makes a face when she sees how dead it is.

"Has it been like this all night?" She punches in her code to clock in.

"Yep and unfortunately this match is almost over, so soon enough it'll be completely dead."

"Ew. That sucks." She glances at her phone. "Oh, wrong. There's a pep rally tonight. I guess they hadn't done one in like ten years. This should start getting lit in like half an hour."

"Well, I leave in like thirty minutes, but yay for you!"

Thirty minutes later, as if on cue, the door starts opening and people start piling in. I shake my head and laugh, looking at Marissa, who's laughing right back.

"Unbelievable."

"When is Patrick coming in?" I stop undoing the apron I'm wearing and realize I may not be able to leave after all.

"He's in the back," Marissa says. "He hadn't had lunch or dinner, so he's eating back there."

"So you don't need me?"

"You can go." She smiles. "Have fun at the party. Live a little!"

The house is quiet. Too quiet. I don't like it. I'm about to text Jagger, but decide against it. This is casual. I can't just text him because I miss him. I gasp at my own thought, setting the mascara down. I miss him. That's okay though because that's normal. He's my roommate and it's quiet. I'm allowed to miss him even though he's not mine to miss. Right? Right. My phone buzzes with a text from Misty telling me she's outside. I pick up my phone and shove it into the crossbody bag I'm wearing, and walk out the door. The moment I step out I shiver. It got chilly.

"It got chilly," I shout out, turning around to see my sister in the back seat of the Uber, a black SUV.

"Hey, Jo," Dylan calls out.

"I'll keep you warm." Bobby lowers the window of the front passenger seat.

I laugh, then look at Misty. "Should I get a jacket?"

"We're going to be inside, so no, you'll lose it. you lose everything." She rolls her eyes, opening the door for me. "Get in, loser!"

"You know, you don't have to say that every time," I say, but laugh anyway, because it is funny. "Hi, guys." I smile and wave at each of them, suddenly feeling shy.

"You look incredible," Bobby says, turning fully in his seat just as the driver starts driving.

"Thank you." I feel myself blush.

The two of them are wearing long-sleeve button-downs and jeans, so I'm assuming this frat party isn't your typical kegger.

I don't ask though, because it doesn't matter. I'm going anyway. They start talking about baseball—or keep talking about it, judging from the murderous glare my sister suddenly has—pretty quickly, and I relax into my seat. I don't understand men. Supposedly all they do is think about sex when they're not fucking us, but instead of focusing their attention on trying to woo us so they can get laid, they're talking about . . . fucking baseball. And Mitch Cruz, no less. I grab my sister's hand and she squeezes it back with a grip that screams *get me the hell out*. Luckily, we arrive at the house and spill out of the car. When I look at the house, I realize this is the house. *The house.* The one I hooked up with Jagger in that first time. My entire body goes hot so I busy myself with what my sister is doing, which is sending Dylan half of the money for the Uber we just took, which makes me roll my eyes harder until Dylan's phone chime and he looks up at her wide-eyed.

"Hey, you weren't supposed to pay for that."

"It's totally fine." Misty smiles, but it doesn't light up her eyes.

I take her hand again. "Let's go find some drinks, yeah?"

"Definitely." We walk toward the house with Dylan and Bobby in tow, but when we reach the door, each of them sidle up next to us and I wonder if this is their way of telling people we're with them. I assume it is. Another reminder of how out of practice I am.

We get drinks, vodka and Red Bull. Bobby points at a cabinet and tells us that's where the good shit is.

"You know someone who lives here?" I ask.

"I live here," Bobby chuckles.

"Oh." Well, shit. "Interesting."

"I can show you my room if you want." He winks. "I'm not saying that as in *let me show you my room and get naked*, I truly mean I can show it to you."

I laugh. "Thanks for clarifying."

"Not that I'd be opposed to you getting naked." He brings a finger up. "I'm just saying, I'm not a douche like that."

"So what kind of douche are you like?" Misty asks. "Just so we're clear."

"I . . ." Bobby lets out a soft laugh. "I totally set myself up for that one."

"Shots," Dylan shouts. A distraction. Bobby shoots him an appreciative smile. My sister and I roll our eyes and sip our vodka.

We take shots.

As we walk around the party, I spot Lawrence and stop breathing, stop walking, stop functioning.

"Oh shit," Misty says behind me.

"Oh shit is right," I say and Misty doesn't even know about the freaking paper he wants me to sign. "Let's go . . . ummm . . ."

"Game room," Bobby says, grabbing my hand. "Ex-boyfriend?"

"Yes."

"What kind of douche is he?"

"The worst one of all. The cheating, manipulating, asshole kind who's about to get paid millions of dollars and knows it."

"Damn." Bobby laughs. "Note to self, don't sign a million-dollar contract yet."

"Your note to self should be don't be an asshole manipulative cheater, but okay." I sigh, glancing around.

We walk down three steps into a room that looks like a total mancave. Huge big screen TV, billiard table in the middle, and two table tennis tables that are currently being used for beer pong. I stop short when I spot Jagger, standing on the other side of the room. There's a girl currently holding on to his arm, looking up at him as she speaks. He's laughing, about to bring the beer bottle in his hand to his mouth when his eyes meet mine. My heart gallops. He takes a sip of his beer, still looking at me as the girl continues to talk to him, her hands still on him. His eyes lower to take me in slowly, and suddenly the tight, short dress I'm wearing makes me feel like I'm naked. His eyes stop at my waist, or I think it's my waist, until I realize my hand is still holding Bobby's. I don't know why, but I let go quickly, as if caught doing something I shouldn't be doing, which is dumb since Jagger has made it clear that we're not serious and I can date other people if I want.

Chapter Twenty-Three

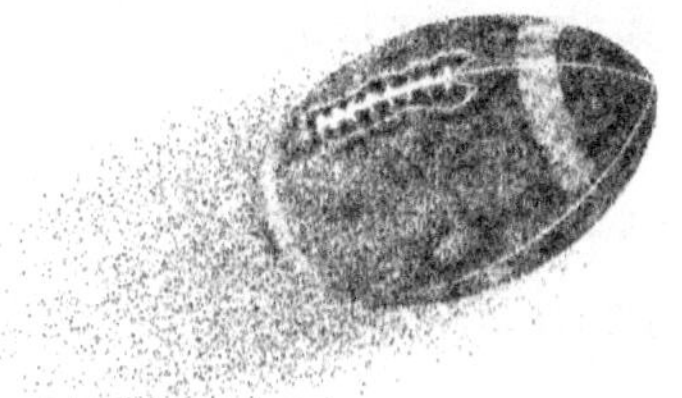

Jagger

'VE BEEN WATCHING JOSEPHINE PLAY BEER PONG AND FLIRT WITH Bobby for five minutes and already I can't stand it. I could be petty and do the same with Cassidy, whose been trying to get in my pants since last year and hasn't left my side the entire time I've been here, but I'm not a petty person. I don't like mind games or wasting precious time. Maybe my first year, or my second, or even my third, but I'm not into the games anymore. I'm also not into fucking multiple women at once. At least, not anymore. Not after I finally had Jo again. Jo, who won't even admit to herself that the reason she won't allow me to fuck her in my bed is because I fucked other women there before her. I don't make it a habit of guessing what people are feeling, but I know Jo and I know that's the case here and from the way she keeps glancing over here and looking between me and Cassidy I also know she's just as bothered by this as I am by seeing her with Bobby. The question is, will she do something about it? Will I?

"Are you going to start next week?" Cassidy asks. I tear my gaze from Jo's and pay attention to Cassidy instead.

"I don't know. Probably not."

"Is your shoulder still hurting?" She brings a hand up and touches my shoulder, doing a massaging motion. It feels good, so I let her continue.

"Sometimes. It depends on my movements."

"Well, if you want to come upstairs with me, I'll do all the work," she says, lowering her voice as she pushes her chest against mine.

I smile because I can't help it. Getting attention from beautiful women is something that I may be accustomed to, but it doesn't mean it gets old, and Cassidy is a ten out of ten, with her curvaceous body and an ass that a Kardashian would pay for. I hold her gaze as I take another sip of my beer. I'm almost out and I'm on a two-beer limit, for no particular reason other than the fact that I know myself and pacing is everything during football season, which means I either get another beer or take Cassidy upstairs and let her ride me, which would make her year and my night. She'd be good in bed. That's not even a question.

I've seen her dancing and I've heard enough from my teammate, Rodney, the backup quarterback, to know she'd be great, but she's not Jo. It's a stupid ass thought. Jo wouldn't care if I took Cassidy upstairs. Still, the thought makes me glance over at her. I find that she's openly staring at me. Her gaze lowered to the hand Cassidy is dragging down my torso and finally sets on the band of my jeans. Jo's eyes flare. She looks up at my face. I raise an eyebrow, like *does this bother you? What are you going to do about it?* She seems to receive the message loud and clear and steps away from Bobby and walks over to me, her hips swinging with each step. I bite my lip, my mouth watering as I think about those hips, those thighs around my waist, that wet cunt squeezing my cock.

"Can I speak to you?" she asks when she reaches me. Cassidy drops her hand and steps back.

"I'll be back." I look at Cassidy.

"Sure." She tries for a smile, but it's shaky and unsure before she turns around to leave. "I'm going to grab a beer."

"You having fun?" I look at Jo again.

"No."

"No?" I chuckle, downing the last bit of beer before setting the bottle on the table beside me. "You looked like you were."

"I want . . . I think we need to talk about our terms."

"Our terms?"

"Can we go somewhere else?" She leans in slightly. "It's loud in here."

It's not that loud in here. The DJ is set up in the living room, but if she wants more privacy, I'll follow her.

"Lead the way." I nod my head.

Josephine starts walking. First she goes toward the living room, but freezes and starts walking down the opposite hall instead. I contemplate whether or not I want to help her out, but decide I don't want to make this easy for her and if I'm being really honest, I'm enjoying the view of her ass in that dress. She stops at the foot of the spiral stairs in the back and looks around for a second. There are people back here too, two different couples making out—two guys on one side and a guy and a girl on the other. I stare at Jo, wondering what her play will be. None of these people will care if we talk here. They haven't looked up at all. Josephine doesn't seem to want any kind of audience though, and starts walking up the stairs. I bite my lip to keep from groaning when I look up and see her black thong. I follow her up the stairs, but there's no silence. Instead of going back downstairs or trying one of the rooms, she pulls me into the bathroom. I stifle a smile as she locks the door behind us, then lean against the counter and cross my arms as I wait, but she doesn't speak, instead she walks over to check behind the curtain and walks back slowly.

"Is this private enough for you?" I ask.

She gives a nod, no humor in her expression, and stands in front of me with her arms crossed across her chest. "I don't want you to sleep with other people."

"What?" I let out a soft chuckle.

"I don't want you to sleep with other people," she repeats.

"I thought you wanted casual?" I ask slowly, searching her hazel eyes.

"I do." She licks her lips. "But I don't like the idea of sharing."

"And this rule extends to you as well?" My heart thunders in my ears. It's taking all the restraint I have to not pull her into my arms and kiss her right now. "You won't sleep with anyone else?"

"I won't."

"Does Bobby know that?"

"I'll make sure to tell him."

"What's brought this on?" I ask even though I know the answer, but I want to hear her say it.

"It's just something I've been thinking about." She shrugs a shoulder, uncrossing her arms. So she's not going to say it. I bite back a smile. "So do you agree?"

"I'm going to need to think about it." It's a lie.

I don't need to think about it. I'm hers. I've been hers for a long time, even though she doesn't know it, but I want her to sweat this out a little. Maybe I am petty after all.

"Okay." She swallows and glances away. "Let me know when you know."

I uncross my arms and widen my stance slightly, reaching for her. She looks at me, wide-eyed, as she steps between my legs.

"I thought about it," I say, bringing a hand up to cup her face, my thumb underneath her chin as I bring her lips closer to mine. "I choose you."

I see the moment something inside of her shifts, the way her eyes widen a bit, the flush that paints her already colored cheeks. Her lips part just before I set mine on hers and her tongue finds mine quickly. My heart races. It's not just that I've had a crush on Jo for as long as I can remember. It's not just that ever since that night we hooked up when we were both freshmen I've fantasized about her. Both of those things are true, yes, but it's more than that. I've never felt this way about anyone before. Even my first girlfriend, who I compared the rest to for a while, pales in comparison to what I feel when Jo and I kiss, when we touch, when we fuck.

It's as though she's painted the grey world I lived in. She's still kissing me as she reaches for the hem of my T-shirt, pulling away slightly to take it off me. She slows as she reaches my shoulder and carefully pulls it over my head, placing it on the counter behind me. Her eyes rake over my body hungrily. It's a look I've seen a million times, but when Jo does it, damn. I let her take the lead in this, reveling in the fact that she wants me this badly. She kisses my neck and works her way down my torso, my abdomen contracting with each lick. When she reaches the waistband of my jeans, she stops and looks up, and I swear I have never seen anything hotter than Josephine Canó crouching between my legs. She unbuttons my jeans, frees my cock, which is already hard for her, and licks from my shaft to the tip. My head falls back. Instinctively, I grip a fistful of her hair in my hand as she continues to lick before covering the head of my cock with her mouth. It takes everything for me to open my eyes and look down on her, but I want to see this, I want to remember this moment for all of eternity. When I'm eighty, I'm going to close my eyes and think about Josephine, my wet dream, sucking my dick at a frat party. I let her do this for a few seconds before gripping her hair and pulling her away because the need to bury myself inside her is too great. She stands up, a fire in her eyes that can only match mine, and I turn her around so that she's facing the mirror. I lean down to run my hands up her legs and meet her gaze in the mirror when I reach the short dress she's wearing.

"Did you wear this for him?"

She swallows, shaking her head.

"For me?" I raise an eyebrow, hiking her dress up slowly until her ass is exposed. She's wearing a black thong that I take a step back to appreciate before I'm on her again, squeezing her ass in my hands.

"I wore it for me," she says, her voice a whisper. "But I was hoping you'd see me in it."

"For what? So I could go fucking crazy?" I bring a hand around her waist and tuck my hand into her thong, resisting the urge to groan as my fingers find her pussy slick, ready, wanting.

She shudders as I touch her folds. Bites her lip as I play with her swollen clit. She keeps her eyes on mine though. I've had sex with a lot of women, but this experience is by far the most erotic.

"Did you think I'd do this?" I lean in and bite the shell of her ear, my fingers still moving on her clit, her folds, spreading her wetness. "Did you think I'd fuck you at this frat party tonight?"

"No," she says, a shaky sigh as she grinds her hips against my hand.

"Did you think I'd just let you walk out of here without having your pussy? Without burying myself so deep inside you that you'd struggle to walk afterwards without thinking of me?"

"Oh God," she breathes as she comes on my fingers.

It's what makes me come undone. I pull down my pants until they're around my knees, roll a condom on quickly, and impale her. She yelps. When I thrust into her again, bringing my hands to her chest, pulling down her dress so that her breasts are exposed, I tweak her nipples in my fingers. She yells out my name. I thrust harder, deeper, tugging her nipples and moving inside her until she's squirming, coming around my cock with a grip that squeezes and makes me start coming as well.

When we finish, we clean up and get dressed. I wait for her to turn to me again and hate how she's trying not to meet my eyes.

"You're beautiful." I cup her face and make her look at me. "You're fucking perfect, Jo."

"So are you." She bites her lip after she says it, bashful and cute as hell.

I kiss her then, a long, languid kiss that makes my heart double in speed. It makes me feel like I'm on the field running to catch one of Jamal's perfect passes, like I'm scoring a touch-down for my team and everyone's cheering for me from the stands. It's enough to scare me a little, because even as I pull away and look down at her, I know I'm fucked. We walk down-stairs holding hands and head to the door, ready to leave. Misty tells us she's going to stay with a friend of hers who's there, and Jo seems to feel comfortable with it because she kisses her sister and the friend on the cheek and takes my hand again. As we walk out, I spot Lawrence looking at us with a frown on his face. I don't know if he's jealous or feels like the ultimate loser for letting Jo go, but it's my turn to smirk at him.

She's mine now, asshole.

Chapter Twenty-Four

Jo

I WAKE UP TO FIND JAGGER STILL SLEEPING BESIDE ME AND I REALIZE that he never left my bed. My heart swells, but it's a fleeting emotion that's quickly replaced with fear. I hate that my past relationship has made me this unsure person that I never was before. I watch the slow rise of his chest as he sleeps and realize that it's better this way. I can't afford to fall for Jagger. Just because he agreed to be exclusive on the sex front doesn't mean he wants something more with me. I think about Jessa and the way she cried that night because he wouldn't make her his girlfriend and turn away from him as I get up to use the bathroom. If he didn't want to take things to the next level with her, why would he with me, with anyone? From my understanding, Jessa wasn't the problem, it was the fact that he truly doesn't want something serious. In that regard, not much has changed from four years ago.

"I don't want a serious relationship," was what I heard him say to Maverick. "I want the college experience."

And that was *after* we slept together. After I lost my virginity to him. I push that thought away. I'd never seen my virginity as something to worship. It was just something I stayed with longer than I thought I would. I respect that about Jagger though. He's never made promises he couldn't keep and I'm grateful that he's always been up front about things like that. My cell phone vibrates on the counter as I'm finishing brushing my teeth. Lawrence's face appears in my line of vision and I instantly feel queasy, but I answer the call.

"I'm outside your house."

"What?" my voice comes out louder than I intend. "Why?"

"Because I need to talk to you." He sighs heavily.

"I'll be right out." I hang up the phone and go back to my room and grab a T-shirt and sweats, pulling them on quickly.

"Why are you in such a rush?" Jagger mumbles from bed. "It's Sunday."

"I just . . . I have to take care of something. Go back to sleep." I rush out of the room and jog to the front of the house, stepping outside before either Jagger has a chance to stand up and follow or Lawrence rings the doorbell.

I freeze when I turn around and find Lawrence standing there, with his hands in his pockets. His blond hair is longer now, the straight strands tucked behind his ears, those clear blue eyes I used to get lost in are looking at me, but I realize that I feel . . . nothing. It's that realization that makes me walk down the steps until I reach him.

"Hey."

"Hey." He rocks slightly. "So . . . you and Jagger, huh?"

I open my mouth to tell him it's not serious, but instead I give a nod. I don't owe Lawrence an explanation.

"So you're definitely over me," he says.

"I guess I am." I keep my gaze on his. "What do you want?"

"The paper, Jo."

"The paper. Of course."

"Well, apologizing again seems futile." He shrugs a shoulder.

"The paper isn't signed yet."

"I don't understand why it's so difficult for you to sign your name on a paper that states you won't divulge secrets of our relationship."

"I don't understand why it's so difficult for you to understand that you're asking me to lie."

His jaw clenches.

I cross my arms.

"What do you want me to do, Jo? I need this done. I want this done. Sign it and we can both move on. If you never want to see me again, this is the perfect segue to that."

I have nothing to say to that, so I glance away, arms still crossed. The morning joggers are out. I focus on them. Overachievers.

"Have you told Jagger?"

"About what?" I meet Lawrence's eyes again.

"About what happened."

"I haven't told anyone about what happened, Lawrence. That should be reason enough for me not to have to sign a damn paper."

"Coach isn't going to let it go and my agent definitely won't let it go."

"Fuck your coach and your agent."

"You're not going to be saying that when my agent starts paying you a visit instead of me."

I glare. "Fuck. Your. Agent."

His jaw twitches again. He glances over my head and fixes on whatever is there. It takes me a minute to realize Jagger probably stepped outside. I look over my shoulder and confirm it. He's standing there wearing athletic shorts and no shirt. His hair is all crazy like he just got fucked, which, isn't not true.

"I guess I'll see myself out," Lawrence says, looking at me again. He looks pissed. His face is blotchy. "Sign the paper."

I wait until he walks away and turns to continue walking down the street before I turn around and make my way back to the house. Jagger's still standing at the door. He holds it open for me and shuts it behind us, locking it before he turns to me.

"You okay?" His eyes are full of concern as they search mine. I nod. "What did he want?"

"To apologize. Again. And for me to sign that stupid paper," I add, my voice a little quieter.

He stares at me for a beat. Waiting. Finally, he simply nods and starts walking to the kitchen. "You want coffee?"

"Sure." I follow him.

We sit down and have our coffee in silence, until he breaks it.

"Do you want to go to brunch?"

My gaze snaps up to his. "Today?"

"Yes today." He chuckles.

"Just me and you?" I frown, wondering if there's some kind of catch. Brunch isn't dinner though, so technically he's not really giving me any special treatment.

"Unless you want to invite someone."

"Sure. I mean, sure to brunch. I have no one to invite unless I invite Misty and she's going home to have breakfast with my mom."

"And you're not?"

"Let's just say I'm not on the best terms with my parents right now."

"Because of the accident?"

"Yeah."

"They can't possibly blame you for it."

I shrug and drink my coffee.

"What really happened with volleyball?"

"What do you mean?" I swallow.

"You loved that sport. You were on the team and you were freaking phenomenal."

"How would you know?"

"I went to some of your games."

"When?" I sit up straighter. This is news to me.

"When my parents came into town. They always wanted to see you play."

"Oh." I frown. "I remember them going, but I don't remember you being there."

"You seemed intent on staying away from me, so I always left and waited in the car when the game was over."

"Oh." I glance away and focus on my nearly empty mug.

"Why was that?"

"Why was what?"

"Why'd you act like you absolutely hated me? I mean, I carried that guilt for a while, thinking maybe I said or did something wrong that night, but . . . man, I've been over it in my head so many times. I don't understand what happened."

"It wasn't you." I met his eyes. "It was . . . it was a me issue."

"So, what happened with volleyball?"

"Do you ask all of the women you're casually fucking for specifics on their lives?" I sit back and keep watching him.

"Only when curiosity gets the best of me." He sits back and mimics my pose, but he's shirtless and all I can see are his muscles.

"Where do you want to go for brunch?" I ask, trying to steer the conversation in another direction. Jagger knows this.

"Anywhere you want to go." His mouth tips up slightly.

"I don't have a preference. I just need to shower and get ready." I stand up. He stays sitting, looking up at me with those toffee eyes that look almost golden today.

"You need help in the shower? I can be very thorough."

A shiver runs down my spine as I set the mug in the sink and start walking away. I look at him before I'm completely out of the kitchen. "I'll leave the door unlocked."

As I'm walking down the hall, I hear him scramble to his feet and smile. I know he's not mine forever, but I'll settle for right now.

Chapter Twenty-Five

Jagger

I WASN'T KIDDING WHEN I SAID I NORMALLY DON'T TAKE GIRLS ON dates and it is apparent in the way I keep glancing over my menu to make sure Jo is still sitting in front of me. Jesus. Why am I so nervous? I've been inside of her, I've had my tongue on every inch of her body, and yet sitting at a restaurant with her is what makes me nervous? We're sitting across from each other in a big booth, so it's not like we're holding hands or anything, and yet, I feel this way.

She sets her menu down and looks at me. "I'm going to have the Cinnamon Toast Crunch pancakes."

"I think I'll have the same." I set my menu down.

"You want to share?"

"Do I want to share?" I chuckle. "Not particularly. If it's too much for you, I'll have the rest."

"Okay." She smiles. "I hate wasting food."

"Same." I smile back. The waitress comes over and gasps.

"Jagger Cruz." She smiles wide. "Long time no see."

"Hm." I smile, nodding. I haven't been here in a while, but I'm not sure if Beth's talking about that or about us hooking up last year, so I keep it simple. "How have you been?"

"Good. Better now that you're here." She's still smiling when she looks at Jo. "Oh. Are . . . is this a date?"

"We're friends," Jo says. "I'd love some coffee and we're both getting the Cinnamon Toast Crunch pancakes."

Beth seems at a loss for a second, but she nods and smiles and takes our menus before walking away.

"Another one of your casualties?" Jo asks.

"My casualties?"

"Casual hookup whose heart you broke."

"Uh, yes to the first one." I rub the back of my neck.

"Are you uncomfortable right now?" She laughs lightly. "I don't think I've ever seen you look uncomfortable."

"I don't think I've ever had to explain myself to anyone. Normally women ask about other women in passing, not . . ." I shake my head. "I've never taken a woman to brunch."

"Why is that?" She leans forward a little, placing her elbow on the table and her head in her hand. "Are you afraid they'll fall in love with you if you give them dick *and* feed them?"

"Why does it sound so ridiculous when you say it?"

"Because it is. It's pretty apparent that your ex-hookups fell for you pretty hard, and you never fed them, so I think there's a flaw in your little plan."

"Is this your way of telling me you're falling in love with me?" My heart hammers. Shit. I really went there.

"No." She scowls. It's the prettiest scowl, her small nose scrunching up like that.

Soon, Beth is back, wordlessly setting two mugs and a pot of coffee on the table for us before walking away. She doesn't even ask if we need anything else. Not that I care. I'm still looking at all the shades of pink Jo's cheeks are turning.

"So, volleyball," I say. She can't escape that subject here. Not unless she flat out says she doesn't want to answer the question and I really hope she does because for some strange reason I want to know.

"No one knows what happened." She keeps her eyes on the mug of coffee she just poured and slides it over to me before pouring one for herself. I lift mine and cheers her as a thank you.

"No one? Your absence is . . . obvious. I'm sure some people know."

"No one knows." She sighs, taking a sip of coffee and setting down the mug, keeping her hands linked around it. "I was in a car accident in the summer and got a DUI." She meets my gaze. "I've never said this aloud." She licks her lips. "My parents got my record expunged. I had to do community service during the summer and then once that was done, they thought it was only fair that I paid them back for the damages."

"It was your dad's car, right?"

"Yeah. The fucking Maserati."

"Ouch." I wait a moment because shit, she totaled that car. "DUI, huh?"

She nods, still looking at her mug and suddenly I understand why she really doesn't want to talk about it. A DUI is a big deal, but for her to get one? I can't even imagine her parents' reactions.

"I don't know if I want to play football anymore." I swallow a gulp of hot coffee and look at her. Her eyes snap up to mine. "My shoulder has been fine for a few weeks now. The PT at UNC says it's fully healed and it is, I know it is, but . . . " I shake my head and say the words I haven't even spoken in front of my brother. "I'm scared."

"Of what?" Jo's frown deepens. "Getting hurt again?"

"Yes. No." I shake my head, letting out a laugh. "I don't know."

Jo doesn't say anything for a beat, and then stands up and walks over to my side of the booth, sliding in. "Scoot."

I scoot, looking at her like she's gone mad.

"Talk to me."

"I . . . am talking to you," I say slowly.

"Why are you scared?" she whispers.

"I don't know. I'm not kidding. I really don't know."

"Are you scared that you'll get hurt so bad that you won't be eligible for the NFL?"

"I . . . " Damn. I suddenly wish I could take back my words and rewind the conversation because I am not ready to talk about this over brunch. "I don't think I want to go pro."

"What?" she blinks. "Why?"

"That's the issue. I don't know *why*. I mean, not exactly anyway. I think this injury opened my eyes to all the others that will come. I guess I don't want to feel like a failure. I don't know. I'm technically not even in my father's shadow since I don't play his sport, and yet here I am." I shake my head, letting out an exhale. "What kind of an athlete doesn't want to go pro?"

"A fake athlete." She nods, pursing her lips. "You're a faker."

I blink.

She laughs, nudging my shoulder with hers. "I'm joking."

"Don't joke like that."

"Stop frowning." She leans in and puts the tips of her fingers to my temple. "You look hot when you frown and I can't kiss you in public."

"You're all over me, Josephine. If you kissed me right now, it would make no difference."

She laughs loudly and looks around. "Shit, am I messing up your game?"

"Completely messing up my game."

"Would you be pissed if I kissed you and someone took a pic?" She searches my eyes.

"Absolutely not."

"Really?" She raises an eyebrow and I realize she's seriously asking me this question.

"Why would I be mad?"

"Lawre—" She stops herself with a shake of her head.

"Lawrence what?"

"He was big on no public affection." She sits straight in her side of the booth, looking forward suddenly. "Of course, that would explain the cheating." She swallows and glances at me quickly. "You were right about that."

"I'm sorry that I was."

"Are you?"

"I truly am. Why would I want you to get hurt?" I frown, then frown more when I realize I almost told her I love her. But I can't. I mean, I don't. *Right?*

"I'm not saying you wanted me to get hurt." She stops talking when Beth brings our food.

Beth, who takes a full, shocked step back when she sees us sitting on the same side of the booth, but doesn't make a comment about it. We start eating and stop talking. After a few bites, she glances up at me.

"I'm sorry I was so mean to you when you warned me."

"I'm sorry I had to warn you." I meet her gaze and set my hand over hers. We look at each other for a long moment before I say, "I thought you were going to kiss me?"

She laughs before leaning in and kissing me quickly, but she keeps her hand beneath mine as we eat—her with her right hand, me with my left, and I find that I don't want to let go. Unlike Lawrence, I don't care who sees me with her. I don't care what they say or assume. I like Jo. I want her more than anyone I've ever wanted before, and yes that thought scares me, but not more than what's going to become of us once this is over. I'm her rebound, after all.

"So did they kick you off the team because of the DUI?"

She yanks her hand from mine and looks at me. "Why do you want to know so badly?"

"I just told you about my shoulder." I raise an eyebrow. "You're going to have to swear not to tell anyone."

"Can we pinky promise?"

I chuckle, holding my pinky out. "Sure."

"I pinky promise I won't tell anyone your deepest, darkest secret." She wraps hers around mine, then raises an eyebrow. "Your turn."

"You need me to say it?"

"Yes." She shoots me an exasperated look.

"I pinky promise I won't tell anyone your deepest, darkest secret." I roll my eyes and pull her hand to my chest instead of dropping it. "Tell me."

"Lawrence was driving that night." She bites her lip, pausing momentarily. "He was driving. We got into an accident and when the cops got there, I took the fall. After, when Coach found out, she . . ." She looks away, tears in her eyes before she blinks rapidly and looks at me again. "She kicked me off the team. I'm not the kind of player they want on their team."

"Why would you . . ." I drop her hand and shake my head. "Why would you take the fall for him?"

"I just did." She shrugs. "He was freaking out and kept going on and on about the NFL and I just did it and he didn't outright ask me to do it, but I felt like he needed me to and I did. It was the right thing to do."

"You lost your scholarship."

"My parents have the money to pay for my classes," she says. "Thankfully."

"You . . . my God, Josephine." I shake my head.

"I know. I'm fine though."

"You're fine?" I shoot her a look. "You are not fine."

"What was I supposed to do? I would have done the same for you."

I pull away. I know it's not meant to be a diss, but I can't help it, I take it as one, because putting me in the same box as Lawrence? I can't. If it would have been me, I would have owned up to my mistake. If it would have been me, I never would have put myself in that situation to begin with. That is what ultimately makes me start brooding. The rest of the time we're there, there's no hand holding or joking around. I focus on my food, pay the bill, and ignore her. She's pissed off too, I can tell, so it doesn't bother me half as much when it's time to leave and she slides out of the booth and doesn't even wait for me to follow.

Chapter Twenty-Six

Jagger

"**I** WILL NEVER UNDERSTAND WHY GIRLS ARE SO SOFT ON guys." I take another swig of my beer. "I mean, we can all agree that Lawrence is a bitch, right? But for him to cheat on her, of all people and her just let him?" I shake my head, shrugging a shoulder. I leave out the part about the DUI and her taking the fall for him because as mad as I am about it, she made me pinky promise I wouldn't say anything and I intend to keep my word. "I just don't get it. He doesn't even deserve to breathe the air she breathes." When I finish talking, I look at both my brothers to find them staring at me with blank faces. "What?"

"You really like her," Mitch says.

"Of course I like her." I frown. "I mean, she's cool and sexy as fuck."

Mav starts laughing first. "You more than like her. Holy shit. Romeo's in love!"

"I am not in love." I point at him. "I never said that.

"You didn't have to." Mitch chuckles, setting down his beer. "Damn, I leave for a little while and my little brother falls in love."

"Fuck you." I look at him, then at Mav. "And you."

"You know Mom invited them over for Thanksgiving," Mav says. "I guess you can break the news to the family there. Wait, unless you want to take that time to propose?"

I shoot him a look. "I'm not proposing and I am not in love. Can we get back to the topic of women being weak?"

"But they're not," Mitch says.

"Of course you say that." I roll my eyes. "Momma's boy."

"You're a momma's boy too," Mitch shoots back, then looks at Mav. "So are you, so don't even think about denying it."

"I would never deny that," Mav argues.

"If she was weak, she would never have broken it off with Lawrence," Mitch says.

"Dude, he did a lot of shit before she broke up with him and I told her about some of the cheating when I saw her."

"Who cares? She left right before he's about to become a super millionaire," Mav says. "A lot of women would have stayed and reaped the benefits of being with a star."

He's not wrong, but I still hate it. I hate that she seems to still want to protect that piece of shit when he doesn't deserve it. He wronged her so many times. He hurt her deeply and I see it every single day even though no one else does.

"I think I'm in love with her," I say, surprising myself, and them, because even though they talk shit, they weren't expecting to hear me actually admit that.

"Damn." Mitch shakes his head.

"Damn." Mav blinks.

"Damn," I whisper.

"And to her you're just a rebound, right?" Mitch asks. I nod.

"Always the bridesmaid," Mav says. We both shoot him a look. "What? Mom always says that to Lily."

"Yeah, because Aunt Lily is literally always the bridesmaid." Mitch chuckles.

"And I've never wanted to be the bride," I say, rolling my eyes when they both laugh uncontrollably. Assholes. "Or the groom, or whatever."

"It does get old though," Mav says. "Having girls use us for our bodies or connections or money or whatever they think they can get by being with us."

"Why do you think I don't fall into it?" Mitch says. "I've been telling you for years. Keep your eye on the prize."

"The prize being football," I say. "Baseball for you."

"The prize being getting a professional contract. Yes."

"You know what I don't understand? Everyone's talking about this big contract he's going to sign. Does that mean he has an agent?" Mav asks.

"That's a good question." I frown, knowing we're not supposed to sign with anyone until we play our last game.

I've met a lot of agents and already have one in mind that I'll probably sign with, but can't until my last game, so we've never gone into that conversation. It's all very platonic for now. Hi and bye, good game, I like what you did there, etcetera. I could have signed last year, but my injury set me back. Damn injuries.

"Maybe he's just talking to an agent, which of course, is also technically illegal, but still. Who would tell on him?"

I purse my lips. He's not wrong. This is why so many people get away with that. It's a stupid rule to begin with. We meet agents all the time, but can't talk about the future or anything that may hint at us doing any kind of business before our last game played. Even if Lawrence is signed, which I doubt he officially is since everyone knows the consequences of that, I would never snitch on him. As much as I can't stand the guy, I wouldn't want to ruin his freaking life. I shake my head. People like Lawrence get away with everything. Some might say the same thing about my brothers and me, but they'd be wrong. We're more privileged than most, and still we'd never get away with half of the shit guys like Lawrence pull. I take a breath and exhale, unwilling to continue thinking about Lawrence.

"Do you think Jo feels the same about you?" Mav asks.

"I'm not sure." There are times when there's no question about it, but that's usually when we're having sex or alone and she actually lets her walls down for a moment, right before she builds them back up and shutters herself away. She used to be such an open book, not this overly cautious bombshell who looks over her shoulder when she walks and thinks twice before speaking. I think about the paper Lawrence keeps trying to get her to sign and feel my blood getting hot again. I know I need to let it go because if I want her to be more than just a casual hookup, I need to put my energy into that and not spend it on my frustration over the situation with her ex. She's obviously trying to let it go. I need to try to do the same.

Chapter Twenty-Seven

Jo

I STARE AT MY PHONE FOR A FULL TEN SECONDS BEFORE ANSWERING the call.

"I thought you were going to come by on Sunday," my mother says, her voice soft, softer than it has been in months when speaking to me.

"I was busy."

"Hm." She pauses. "When will you not be too busy to see your mother?"

"When my mother stops acting like I killed someone."

"You could have, Jo."

I shut my eyes. *No, I couldn't have,* but my mother doesn't know that and honestly I'm not sure that she ever will. It wouldn't make a difference anyway. It's not like I'd be able to play this last season of volleyball because even if I came clean to my parents, I would never come clean to my coach or old teammates. I truly didn't want to hurt Lawrence, despite every-thing. Maybe in a few years I'd tell people the truth about what happened, and who would even care at that point? Besides, as far as I'm concerned, my teammates don't deserve my friend-ship. Not after the way they cast judgment and never even tried to keep in touch after I was kicked off the team. I get it, I do, drunk driving is absolutely unacceptable, but I wasn't driving. It's the freaking reason I wasn't driving. Lawrence had nothing to drink that night, yet still lost control of the vehicle.

"I don't want to talk about this, Mom," I say after a long bout of silence.

"Fine. The Cruzes invited all of us to hang out next week-end. A Friendsgiving of sorts."

"Football season is on."

"It's next weekend. Jagger will be on bye week."

"Already?"

"I don't make the football schedule."

"Are we driving or flying?"

"Driving. We're going to Asheville, not New York."

"Oh."

"Are you going to come? I know you always say no, but I figured I'd ask and I need to tell Milly so she can be ready for us."

"Yeah, I'll go."

"Good." Mom pauses. "I hope to see you before then, but if not, I'll text you the information, unless you want to ride with us?"

"I'll ride with Misty."

"I haven't spoken to her yet," Mom says. "I don't know if she's going."

"She'll go."

"Okay. Sort that out and get back to me. I love you, Josephine. Even if you don't come visit me."

"I love you too, Mom."

When we hang up, I feel bereft. I truly miss my mother, but I can't deny that I'm still pissed at her. Not because she punished me or for taking away the car they gave me for my high school graduation. I'm mad because she never let me explain myself to her or make things right. They just blew the entire thing out of proportion because they didn't want to look like bad parents, so it was *get a lawyer, expunge the DUI, pay this person and that person, oh, and after you're done with community service, clean the practice once a week.* I wasn't even mad at all of it. On a deep level, I understood what they were doing. I was just hurt.

I think about Jagger now and wonder what he must think of me. I never gave him a chance to question me. After our brunch non-date fiasco, we've pretty much stayed away from each other. I hear him when he gets home late at night after practice and sometimes he's already there, playing Madden with his friends, when I get home from the bar. He hasn't so much as looked at me for more than two seconds. Every time he does, I can tell he's mad though and that's enough for me not to want to speak to him. I'm tired of having people be mad at me for no reason and I'm even more tired of having to explain myself to them.

Chapter Twenty-Eight

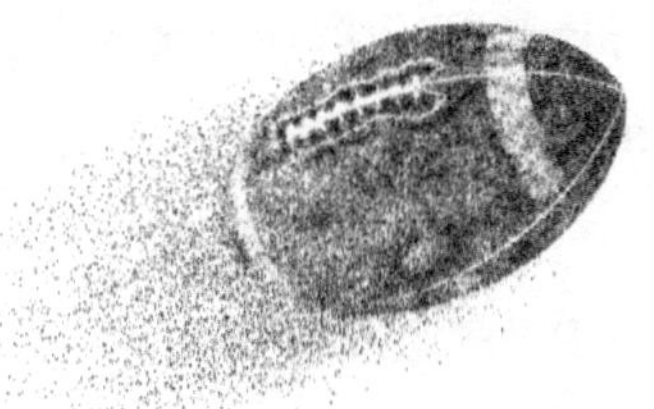

Jagger

"CUT LEFT. CUT LEFT!" COACH B SCREAMS.

I cut left, but it's too late, Payton throws the ball over my left arm and I have no time to catch it. I throw my hands down and curse.

"Dammit, Cruz!" Coach B yells again. "You keep that up and you won't be starting on Saturday."

I shut my eyes and exhale, taking the bottle of the sports drink the water boy is handing me as Payton walks over.

"You good?" he asks.

"Miscalculation." I shake my head and squirt the drink into my mouth before throwing the bottle down on the ground. "Fuck."

"You think you'll be ready by Saturday?"

"Yes."

"You know the plays. You just need to execute."

"I fucking know that, Pay." I shoot him a look.

"What play do you want me to run that's going to make you catch the fucking ball and score?" he asks.

Most QBs I've played with wouldn't ask that. They'd be quick to replace me because they don't trust I can get the job done. Payton and I have been friends since freshman year and even though I was a starting tight end when I got here, he had to warm the bench until our last QB left for the NFL. Still, he's been the one I vibe with most when it comes to his impeccable throwing. His arm has power and precision, two things I can count on. Normally, playing with him is easy and seamless, but after my injury, nothing has felt that way.

"Let's just run that one again," I say, picking up the bottle I'd thrown on the ground and handing it to the water boy.

We run the route again. This time, I'm there, but don't lift my arm. I cover my face with my hands. It's frustrating because I envision myself catching the fucking ball every time, and when it comes down to execute the play, I freeze. I'm scared. There's no way around it. I'm terrified I'll pull a ligament. Terrified I'll undo the work I've put in to repair my shoulder. If I keep at it, they won't start me and before I know it, I'll lose my spot. I know this just as well as they do. Coach jots something down and it takes everything in me not to scream.

"What are you going to do when you have someone tackle you?" Coach B asks. "You going to freeze up and let them take the ball?"

"Fuck." I take a deep breath. "No. I can do this."

"Let's get Jarvis out here," Coach says. "And Philip."

My eyes go wide. Coach shrugs like he's not trying to kill me out here. Fullbacks Jarvis and Philip don't take it easy on anyone, not even me. With good reason. We're here to dominate, not fuck around. I was always grateful for the way they put their hearts into practice because I knew nothing could mess me up in the actual game, but now? Now I'm fucking petrified. I stare at them as they jog over to the field. They're both going pro, no doubt, and I'll be proud of them for it as long as they don't kill me out here.

"Let's go, twinkle toes," Jarvis says, grinning.

"Fucker." I narrow my eyes.

"You need to toughen up," he shoots back. "They're not going to take it easy on us this weekend."

I nod. He's right. They're all right. It doesn't make it any easier though.

"Come on, Cruz. You can outrun us easily. Outrun us with the fucking ball in your hand," Philip adds.

Jamal sets up. The rest of us follow suit—Phil and Jar ready to double team me, and me ready to catch the damn ball and run like hell. Payton lifts the ball in his hand and rocks back. I start running the route, cutting left, Payton launches the ball as Jarvis and Philip rush me. I catch it, cradle it, and run like hell. They're right on my tail, I hear both of them practically breathing on me, but it doesn't matter. I make it past the touchdown line and throw my hands up.

"You always work well under pressure." Jarvis bumps my fist with his.

"Let's go again," that's Coach B. "Bring out the rest of the team."

"Coach . . ." Tucker's eyes widen. "We already practiced with Jordan."

"And now you're all going to do it again together." Coach shoots him a pointed look. "Or are you here to make jokes and perform the entire *Hamilton* musical?"

"No, sir." Tucker looks at his feet. Payton, Jarvis, and I stifle a laugh.

Tucker's been singing that damn musical for two years now and today's practice has been no different. This time, when the team comes back, Jordan also joins us on the field. He looks at me as if making sure I'm good and ready, and I give him a nod. Fear or no fear, I was born ready.

Chapter Twenty-Nine

Jo

"ARE YOU GOING TO THE GAME TODAY?"

I swivel around to see Jagger standing in the threshold of the kitchen. He's wearing sweat pants and a Giants t-shirt. I haven't seen him in days and it feels like weeks, and I realize that I miss him. I miss his lips on mine and his hands exploring my body. I miss talking to him, too. I just . . . miss him. I swallow back those emotions because casual and missing someone don't go hand in hand.

"I work."

He nods once before walking into the kitchen and going to the coffee maker.

"You've been busy lately," I say.

"So have you." He doesn't look up at me when he says that.

I've been busy trying to avoid him more than anything.

The whole casual thing isn't working for me anymore and I don't want to be yet another girl who falls for Jagger, but it's hard not to. I also don't want to be Jessa in this situation, who brings it up and then is tossed aside for good. I need time to think about this and if it takes me all week, it takes me all week. I already decided that I need to officially cut all of my loose ties. I'll forgive what needs to be forgiven and move on from Lawrence for good. I'll come clean to my mother about the accident and make her swear not to make a big deal out of this. I'll figure out where Jagger and I stand and how to cut him loose if we're not on the same page. I just can't handle anything that will lead to more regret right now.

"At what time do you get off work?" He stirs some cream into his coffee and meets my eyes.

"Seven."

"What are you doing after?"

"I have to take care of something and then nothing." I shrug a shoulder.

"Jordan's having a party."

"So you'll be busy tonight." I offer a small smile and hope it's not shaky.

I would offer more, but I agreed to dinner with Lawrence tonight so that I can finally give him the signed paper and put everything behind us for good. Dinner at the bar, so there's no confusion about it. He'll come right after my shift, we'll have dinner and talk, I'll give him a revised version of the NDA, signed, and then we're absolutely done. I added a clause that says I won't talk to reporters or write a tell-all about our relationship, but that doesn't mean I have to keep his name out of my mouth if someone asks me a direct question that I actually want to answer.

"I can text you the address if you want," Jagger says, but he's so nonchalant that I get the feeling maybe he doesn't want me to go at all but is extending the invite just to be nice. *Casual. Casual. Casual.* I say that in my head three times and try to seriously push down how much I'm dying for him to kiss me.

"Okay," I say instead.

"No pressure." He shrugs a shoulder. "But if you want to go . . ."

"Maybe I can stop by." I smile. He starts walking out of the kitchen, but stops when I speak again. "How's your shoulder feeling? Have you been stretching it?"

"Yep. Following my doctor's orders." He winks as he walks away.

We never finished our conversation at brunch the other day and I haven't seen much of him at all this past week. I feel like a total ass about the way I walked out of that restaurant, too. It's not like Jagger doesn't have a million and one people to talk to about his problems, but he chose to tell me that day and I chose to walk away, so it's my fault things are weird between us now. I've been avoiding him mostly because I don't know how to act around him, but I figured once I saw him again things would be cool, totally normal. Obviously, I was wrong. I hate it. Jagger walks back out of his room, bringing a duffel bag with him and my heart slams into my chest. I know it's just a bag and he has a game, but it makes me think about the day we moved in and suddenly I get sad knowing that this too will come to an end. I must be wearing my emotions on my face because he stops walking and looks at me, those toffee eyes all concerned.

"You okay?"

"Yeah. Totally fine." I nod and swallow. "I feel like I owe you an apology for how I reacted the other day."

"You don't."

"Right, but I feel like I do." I bite my lip. "You opened up and I was so caught up in my own shit and . . . " I inhale and exhale heavily. "I'm sorry."

"It's fine. Truly." He smiles, but it's not that carefree, joyous smile I've gotten used to and it pains me.

"I would say I can make it up to you with dinner or something, but I know you don't do dinner and casual."

"I don't." He shrugs a shoulder. "Dinner might be nice though." He glances at his fitness watch and back at me. "I'll see you later."

"Good luck." I rush behind him, following him to the front door. I want to kiss him. I want to hug him. I want to apologize again and talk things out. Instead, I stand there, even as he turns to face me and looks at me like he's waiting for more. "I hope you kick ass. I'll be watching from the bar."

"Thanks." He smiles again, another polite one I can't stand and then he's gone.

All I can do is shut the door behind him and lean against it, my emotions clawing at me because I know I've messed up and I don't know how to fix this or if there's anything to fix at all. He said dinner would be nice, but does that mean dinner would be nice because we're no longer going to hook up? Or because he's open to something more? Ugh. I hate not knowing.

Chapter Thirty

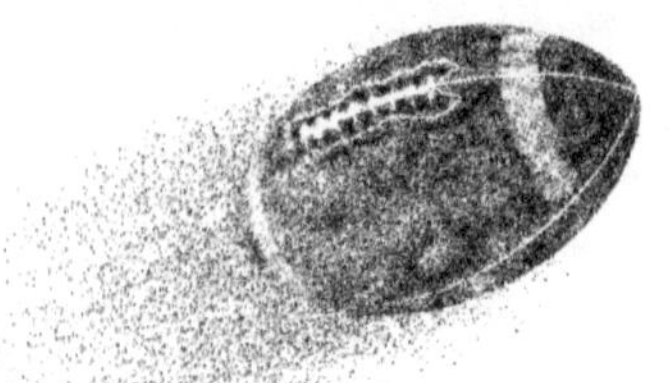

Jagger

NOT ONLY DID WE WIN, BUT WE CRUSHED THEM, 28-7. TWO OF those touchdowns scored by me. The guys are still laughing and slapping each other on the back when we get out of the locker room after showers and stretches. Coach B asked us to meet him back in the room they newly assigned to reporters. When we get there, it's been cleared of reporters and we all take a seat in the ones they vacated. Coach B is standing up front with the rest of the coaching staff, who are all smiling and talking amongst themselves. Adrenaline is still pumping through me as Coach starts talking about the game and I find myself glancing down at my phone to look at the time. Jo gets off work soon, but she still hasn't texted me back about the party after I sent the address. I wanted to tell her to come with me, to invite her as my date, but thought better of it. She's been acting weird and obviously needs her space so I'm trying to give it to her.

"Cruz, you going to join us or keep daydreaming?" Coach B asks. I snap my attention to him as my teammates laugh.

"Sorry, Coach."

"You showed up today. I know you've been worried about your arm, but you played like you were fearless. That's what we need to see out there," he says. "We have a bye next week, but we're still practicing Monday through Thursday. You're dismissed. Go have some fun but not too much fun," he calls out as we file out of the room, all of us collectively buzzing.

"Jordan, can my girl bring her sorority sisters tonight?" Jarvis asks. "They're all hot."

"I can vouch for that," Tucker adds.

"Then hell yeah, bring them," Jordan says. He looks over at me. "You're coming, right?"

"I wouldn't miss it."

"Is Jo coming?"

"I'm not sure." I look at my phone again. "Maybe."

"Bro, have you even talked to her? Told her how you feel?"

"No." I purse my lips, regretting the night I was playing Madden with the guys and spilled my guts to them. It felt good at the time to get things off my chest to someone other than my brothers, but now I have a lot more than just two people pointing out the mistakes I'm making and it's driving me crazy.

"You should."

"You're just saying that because you don't want more competition with the chicks at school." I glance over at him as he laughs.

"You're not competition. You just happened to get to Jo first and I'm not a dick like Lawrence."

His name makes my blood boil. It's funny how we used to hang out and talk all the time and it all died the moment he turned around and went after Jo. Some would say I could also place the blame on her, but she didn't know how I felt. Hell, I didn't know how I felt. I knew I liked her, but in hindsight I don't know that it would have made a difference back then. I'd just gotten here and I truly did want the college experience. I didn't want to get in a relationship with the first girl I had a fling with. Now, years later, I haven't had any kind of relationship with anyone and part of me wonders if it's because of that night with Jo and another part of me thinks it's just because it's too easy to hook up with girls and be done, as opposed to being tied down and having a relationship dictate my every move. It doesn't matter. I'm ready now. I just don't know if she is. She just got out of a bad one and I don't know if she'd want to jump into one with me. She specifically said no athletes and I'm in the thick of it. I say bye to my teammates and sit in my car for a moment to gather my thoughts, but before I can finish gathering them, my phone buzzes with a call from Maverick. I answer.

"Yoooooo," he says loudly, and I can't help but to smile. "What a game. That first touchdown? One-handed catch with two people all over you? Holy shit, that's going to be all over ESPN!"

"It might be." I chuckle, heart pounding at the thought. I've been featured before, but it never gets old.

"Come to the bar," Mav says. "I'm here with Colson and Finn."

"Jordan's party is tonight. I need to shave and take a nap and hopefully eat a bowl of pasta," I add after my stomach grumbles. I showered after the game, but I couldn't shave and I can't stand this weird stage my facial hair is in so I want to get rid of it.

"Dude, I'll order you a bowl of spaghetti. Come on. You can nap after you eat."

"Fine." I exhale and hang up the call.

On the ride over, I wonder if Jo is still there or if she already went home. If she's there, I'm going to be straight up with her and tell her I want her to go with me to the party. If she's not, I'll tell her at home. Either way, this ends tonight. I'm tired of hiding my feelings from her. I need to step up and tell her and be done with it. If she feels the same, it would be amazing. If she doesn't, I can move on once and for all. When I park at the bar, I see her gold Celica and smile. She's still here. I walk inside and spot my brother and his friends quickly, but as I'm walking over, I see Jo sitting in a corner table with Lawrence. I feel myself frown as I slide into the booth, facing her.

"What the fuck is going on over there?" I say, not even bothering greeting anyone.

"Oh." Mav looks over his shoulder and back at me. I continue staring at Jo. "They've been having dinner for a while now."

I shake my head, my jaw tensing. I swear I don't understand this woman. I don't understand why she continues to give Lawrence the time of day. What's the point? I wish I could shake that into her, but it's obvious she wouldn't listen.

"Hi." I glance back at my brother's friends. "Sorry, I'm distracted."

"Beer's on me," Finn says, smiling. "You earned it after that game."

"Jagger Cruz." At the sound of my name, I look up to see a man standing there with a smile on his face. "You played a heck of a game today."

"Thank you, sir." I smile.

"This bar was rooting for you, everyone hollerin'. I wish you could have seen us."

"I appreciate that. It was definitely a good game to kick off the season with."

"You keep playing like that. Keep up the good work." He winks and walks away.

"You're famous," Colson says, showing me his phone. "You're all over Bleacher Report and ESPN right now."

"You're going to go pro," Finn adds. "I mean, most definitely going pro."

"No shit he's going pro," Mav says, pride filling his voice. "Wait till the season is over and the agents start calling."

On that note, my gaze swings back to Jo and Lawrence. I can't see much from here, but I do see his hand on hers and it makes my blood boil. Is she thinking about taking him back? After everything? What would I do if she did? I'd have to move out. No question about it. They stand up and walk toward the back exit together, his hand on her shoulder. I ball my fists and stand up, but before I can take a step in that direction, Mav is in front of me, pressing a hand on my chest.

"Let her go." His voice is low, but clear, and I'm forced to look into his dark brown eyes. "Let it go, Jag. She's choosing to go with him. If she didn't want to, she'd tell him to fuck off and leave."

I swallow. It feels like there's a brick in my throat, but I try to focus on regaining control of myself.

"This is your last season. You can't risk it because of an asshole like Lawrence."

I shut my eyes briefly. I would risk it for her, but my brother's right, if she didn't want to leave with him, she wouldn't have. If she minded him touching her, she'd say so. I think that's what kills me the most. After everything, she'd still choose him.

"Why don't you stay at my place?" Mav asks. "That way you can both have some space."

I nod, still not trusting myself to speak. Then, I get shit-faced. Then, I let my brother drive me to Jordan's party and that's the last thing I remember about that night.

Chapter Thirty-One

Jo

'M LAUGHING AT MARISSA'S PORTRAYAL OF THE LATEST *GREY'S Anatomy* episode when Misty walks into the bar, stomping over like a woman on a mission.

"What happened to you?" I turn to her. Marissa does as well. Misty is seething.

"Did you see the video of Jagger?" Misty asks.

"On ESPN? Yeah," I breathe out. "It was beyond impressive, honestly. Why?"

"I'm not talking about ESPN." She rounds the bar and stands beside us, practically shoving her phone in my face. "This."

I take the phone and look at the paused video on the screen of her phone. I click play and see it come to life, loud music, dim lights, a girl straddling a guy on a couch. She's dancing to the music, but they're clearly making out, his hands gripping her ass. My pulse starts to quicken, then slow way down, as if time itself may pause just for this feeling to fully envelop me. The person holding the cell phone moves to the side and starts saying Jagger's name. The woman on top of him pulls away slightly and sticks her tongue out to the camera. Jagger also looks, no smile, no laugh, just looks straight into the camera. He looks beyond drunk. I've never seen him that way. My stomach squeezes. I set my hands over it suddenly regretting the greasy breakfast I had this morning. I'm going to be sick. I won't throw up. I know myself, but still, the feeling sits in my stomach.

"This was last night?" I whisper.

"Jordan's party."

"Were you there?" I look at my sister. She nods, her eyes filled with pain, but not nearly as much as what I'm feeling.

"Wow," I whisper, walking away to hold on to the counter. "Just. Wow."

"I'm sorry," Misty says. "I know you said casual, but, still, I'm sorry."

"Did he . . . did they . . . "

"I don't know." Misty bites her lip. "They went upstairs together shortly after I saw them."

"God." Tears burn my eyes, and even though I want to be the bigger person and not cry over this, I can't help it. It hurts so much.

"Did you break it off with him?" Marissa asks softly, standing beside me on one side as my sister stands on the other.

"No." I shake my head. "I mean, we haven't hooked up since last weekend, but he's been busy and I've been . . . I was just . . . I don't know." The tears start falling. My sister hugs me with one arm.

"I'm so sorry, Jo."

"Why does this keep happening?" I whisper. "What is wrong with me?"

"Nothing." She pulls away and holds my arms. "Nothing is wrong with you. They're the ones losing out here. Look at me, Josephine." I lift my head up and look at my sister through blurry eyes. "His fuckup has nothing to do with you. It has everything to do with him and his own insecurities. Do you understand that?"

I nod, swallowing past the knot in my throat, and wrap my arms around her as I start to cry again. What I had with Jagger was casual, we said that from the beginning, but when I replay what I saw in that video I feel like I'm being ripped apart inside. What Lawrence did hurt and hurt even more because he cheated with Crystal, who I thought was my friend. When I realized he'd cheated multiple times with different women, I felt like crap and while I wondered what was wrong with me, it didn't feel like this. Maybe it's because it happened with back-to-back guys. Maybe it's because I trusted Jagger in a way I didn't trust Lawrence, because Jagger was vocal about his disgust for cheating, because I know Jagger's parents and know they raised him better than this.

"Maybe he thought you weren't serious about him?" Marissa asks, her voice still soft. "Maybe you can still work this out."

"We agreed to not sleep with other people." I wipe my

tears and take a deep breath as I pull back from my sister and let go. "But I guess we were done." I take another really deep breath. It felt like we may have been done when I saw him earlier, and when he didn't make it a point to talk to me this week, but I didn't expect to find out like this.

"Do you want me to finish up here? I can get Patrick to come in," Marissa says.

"I'm fine." I shake my head. "Thank you."

"Come to my apartment," Misty says. "After work, come straight to my place. I'll go get some of your things while you're here so you don't even have to see him for now."

I nod gratefully and let my sister do this for me. I hate asking for help, but I'm tired of feeling alone.

Chapter Thirty-Two

Jo

NSTEAD OF CLEANING DAD'S PRACTICE AFTER HOURS, I MANAGE TO convince him to let me go in at five in the morning. It's either that or risk running into Jagger and I just can't right now. When I'm leaving, feeling spent from the lack of sleep and the early cleaning, I turn the key to turn on my car and am met with a stalling sound. Again, I turn the key, and again, the car sounds like it's having a coughing fit. I bang my head against the headrest. Of course. Of course the car would break down on me now. I scroll through my phone, trying to figure out who to call. I finally settle on my mom. Dad's in surgery today, otherwise, I'd wait for him. Misty's probably getting ready for class. Mom's probably getting out of her morning Pilates class, which is the main reason I know she'll be able to make it here the fastest. When she pulls up, parking her G Wagon beside me, I break down in tears. It's the exhaustion. I know it is, but still.

"Oh, sweetie." Mom runs over and wraps her arms around me. "I didn't know this car would give you this many problems."

"It's the first time it happened." I wipe my tears. "I'm just tired."

"You worked a late shift last night," she says, pulling away to take her phone out and call AAA.

I realize I could have done it myself, but it doesn't matter. I don't want to be alone anyway. Once she's done on the phone, she tells me to get in her car and we start driving.

"What's wrong?" she asks. "Don't tell me it's just exhaustion. I can see that something else is wrong."

"Nothing." I lean my head against the window. "I really am just tired."

I'm tired and tired of the bullshit.

She's quiet for a moment. "Why don't you stay over on Thursday so we can get an early start on our trip?"

"I don't think I want to go." I glance over at her.

"You're going." She shoots me a look. "I told you to tell me with time, so now you have to go. You need to learn that your words mean something and when you say you're going to do something you need to follow through."

"Fine. I'll go." I cross my arms, feeling like the child she sees me as.

"Where do I take you?" she asks suddenly. "Home? Campus?"

"Oh." I sit up straight. "Campus."

"I can't believe you haven't invited me over."

"Mom, we haven't even been on speaking terms."

"Until you need something." She shoots me another look.

"Well, I'm so sorry for inconveniencing you today, Mother. I'll note not to call you next time." I lean against the headrest and close my eyes.

"I didn't mean for you to take it like that," she says quietly. "I'm sorry."

"It's fine." I open my eyes and look at her, hating the sting I feel in them. "I just wish you guys would have given me some credit."

"Credit for what, Josephine? What you did was reckless. You could have gotten yourself killed." She has tears in her eyes when she finishes that sentence. "I would die if something happened to you, and that is not hyperbole. You're my daughter and one of my best friends. I cannot, will not, live this life without you in it, so excuse me if I felt like I needed to teach you a lesson."

I swallow the lump in my throat and look away, wiping my tears, but they don't stop. At all. Before I know it, I'm full-on bawling in my mom's car and I really don't understand why. Maybe it's the release I needed after holding in all of my emotions. Maybe it's her words that really got me. I don't know, but I can't stop crying. My mom pulls over on the side of the highway, the car shaking slightly as cars zip by us. She throws her arms around me and pulls me to her, and I cry onto her slender shoulder.

"Why don't we go home and I make you a cup of tea?" Mom says against my hair. "Skip class for the day."

I pull away, wide-eyed. "The Dean of Education is giving me permission to skip class?"

"Don't be a brat." She laughs, wiping my tears. "I'm going to call Larsa and let her know I'm going to be in late today and you, young lady, are going to stay at home until we leave for Asheville."

The look she gives me leaves little room to argue, and to be honest, I don't want to. I'm not big on asking for help, but I'd be an idiot to turn down my mother's warmth when I need it most. When we get to her house, she makes good on her promise and makes us tea as she speaks to the people picking up my car from Dad's practice. She sets a mug in front of me and sits down across from me with a sigh.

"So, what's going on with you?"

"Not much." I smile, picking up the mug shakily and taking a sip before setting it down and looking up at her. "I need to tell you something."

"I'm listening." She sets her mug down as well.

"I didn't crash Dad's car."

"What are you talking about, Josephine?" She searches my eyes.

"Lawrence crashed the car that night." I bite my lip.

"But you were drunk. They did a breathalyzer."

"I was drunk, but I wasn't driving drunk."

"Was Lawrence drunk?"

"No. It's why he was driving." I look down at my mug.

"Why wouldn't you tell us this? Why would you take the

fall for it?" She's shaking her head as if trying to understand something that I can barely wrap my head around some days.

"Lawrence has a bright future—"

"So do you," Mom says, interrupting me. "Thank God your father and I could afford a good lawyer and were able to sweep this under the rug, but do you think anyone in your situation would be afforded that luxury? And what if we hadn't been able to actually pull it off? You'd have that on your permanent record for life. That's a big deal, Jo. Your future could have easily been jeopardized because of that boy."

"I made the choice." I swallow. "Lawrence didn't make me take the fall for him. I made that choice myself, so don't blame him."

"I am absolutely not blaming him for your actions. I'm just . . ." She sighs heavily. "I wish you'd told me."

"You were so hell-bent on the lawyer and the car that I just didn't even think it would make a difference. I mean, I wasn't even sure you'd believe me." I bite my lip hard to keep from crying. It doesn't work.

"I always, always believe you, Jo." Mom reaches over and puts her hand over mine. "You are my priority. Not some quarterback or whoever else comes along. You're my daughter. I will always believe you."

"Thanks." I swallow, using my free hand to wipe my tears. "I'm sorry I didn't tell you."

"I'm glad you did now."

"I don't want you to do anything. To Lawrence, I mean. I just want to put this behind me once and for all."

"I don't agree with that, but I respect it. As far as I'm concerned, it's behind us." She squeezes my hand. "Now we need to solve the car situation."

She winks as she lets go of my hand. We spend the rest of the day talking about funny stories she has of students who have come to see her and later, share a bottle of wine with Dad and Misty. It's the happiest I've felt in a while.

Chapter Thirty-Three

Jo

"THIS IS ALL YOU'RE TAKING?" MISTY NUDGES THE DUFFEL BAG on the floor of my teenage room with the tip of her designer sneaker.

"We're only going to be there until Sunday." I frown. "Why? What did you pack?"

"Clothes. More clothes than you." She looks at my bag again, then at me. "Did you pack going-out clothes?"

"Going-out clothes?" I laugh. "For Asheville? Have you been there? Where would we go? A dive bar? A brewery? I have jeans and sneakers or jeans and sandals. Trust me, I'm good."

"Maybe I overpacked." She purses her lips.

"I'd bet money you did."

"I'm surprised you're going."

"I'm surprised you're going." I raise an eyebrow.

"I wasn't going to, but then I found out you were going and I didn't want to leave you alone over there with those wolves." She scowls. "Is he going?"

"Is he going?" I ask at the same time. "Which he are you talking about?"

"Jagger."

"Oh." I shrug, feigning nonchalance, though it's almost not a feign. I've rehearsed what it'll be like to see him again and I think I'm good. "I don't know. Is Mitch going?"

"Nope. I have it on good authority that he got snowed in and had to stay back in New York." She winks.

"Who'd you hear that from?"

"I sent him a text and asked." She shrugs a shoulder.

"Oh, you're texting now?"

"Not texting, per se. We have texted though." She pauses, glancing away briefly. "And we followed each other on social again."

"Wow." My brows shoot up. "I still haven't re-installed any of those apps. I deleted them in case I felt tempted to look at what Lawrence is doing."

"Do you care what he posts?"

"Not anymore." I shake my head. I don't, but Jagger? My stomach hurts just thinking about seeing him. I don't know how I'm going to survive this weekend.

"Jagger hasn't posted in a while," my sister says softly.

"He also hasn't texted." I look up at her, hating the burning feeling in my eyes. "I mean, I haven't been home in a week and he hasn't even called to check in on me. As a friend, you know?"

"He's a dick."

"He *is* a dick."

"Girls, let's go," Dad calls out from somewhere in the house, and I hop out of bed, grab my duffel, and rush behind Misty.

The last time one of us made Dad wait, he made sure we heard about it for months. I am not going to be responsible for that again. I'm trotting down the stairs, trying to go as fast as I can, when I hear his laughter. His laughter. I stumble on the last step, my duffel caught between me and the large wooden post. Misty shoots me a *what the heck is happening?* look and I shoot it right back.

"Girls, put your things in the van. Let's go."

"What van?" I frown. "We don't have a van."

"I rented one." He shoots me a quick *stop wasting time* look before walking back outside.

Misty and I walk outside slowly, shocked, and see a big black van parked there. Not a regular van. No. This looks like one of those party buses you rent for a graduation or a bachelorette party.

"Does this van come with a stripper pole?" I ask, forgetting we have company, and quite frankly, past the point of caring.

Maverick laughs loudly. Jagger does not laugh. I'm not even sure if he's smiling because I refuse to look in that direction. I walk forward, let my father take my bag, then Misty's ridiculous suitcase, and walk inside the van and straight to the back. If I'm going to share a space with Jagger, it's not going to be a close encounter. Misty follows, plopping down in the row in front of me.

"Are we expecting fifteen more, Dad?" she shouts.

"Settle down, girls. This was all they had."

"We could have driven in separate cars," I say, looking down at the ground as Maverick and Jagger climb into the ridiculous vehicle. One of them shuts the door to the back and Mom shuts the door to the front and claps.

"We're off," she announces proudly. "This will be fun."

"Yeah, a ball." I kick off from the floor when Dad starts driving and lie down across the four seats I have to myself. "It's like going to Disney without the excitement."

"Stop talking, Josephine, or I'll drop you off wherever it is you're living right now," Dad warns.

I roll my eyes. "I'd gladly stay there."

"Gladly shut up please."

I shut my eyes and stop talking. After a while, I pull out my phone and open my Kindle app. I haven't read a book in a while and this seems like the perfect time to catch up on my favorite historical romance series. Misty is taking a nap in the row in front of me and I don't think either of us anticipate stopping at all for a three-hour car ride. I mean, we've gone down to Orlando and only stopped once, I can't imagine he's thinking of stopping for this. Despite my nerves and hearing Jagger's voice ring out while he's talking to his brother and my parents, I'm able to get lost in my book. That's huge considering that his voice is cutting and his laughter? God, his laughter is making me feel like I'm drowning. But it's fine. I'm fine. If I survived Lawrence, I can survive Jagger.

I must have fallen asleep at some point because when the van stops moving, I notice and finally open my eyes. I swallow, sitting up and fixing my hair, which I straightened this morning, so it's parted down the center and pin straight up to my elbows.

"Are we there already?" I ask.

"No. We stopped at Cracker Barrel."

I rub my eyes and groan. "Why?"

"I love Cracker Barrel. Come on, girls," Dad says.

And dammit, I should have totally predicted this. My dad always stops for this damn chain. Between this, Bojangles, and Waffle House it's a wrap. Forget the fact that normally he's on a restrictive low carb, high fat, organic as heck diet. I groan again as I get up and stretch my arms over my head and sideways. Unfortunately, for a second I forget who else is sharing this vehicle with me, and when Jagger stands up and glances in my direction, our eyes meet. My heart kicks into gear, thumping at my neck, my ears. He keeps staring and I swear I see anger in his eyes. Anger. It's enough to make me want to scream at him, punch him in the gut. I do neither of those things. Instead, I swallow and force myself to look away. It's not that he's not worth my pain. It's not that he's not worth my rage. It's that I can't have this conversation right now, not in front of my freaking parents, who don't have a clue what's going on. All of us walk out of the van and over to the restaurant, where we're told to wait fifteen minutes. I start walking around in the little store. I love a good store. Soon, Misty joins me, and then my mom, who already has an apron and cast iron pan in her hands. We're called to our table and I realize that Jagger makes it a point to let me pick a seat before choosing one on the opposite end of the table. He's avoiding me. He's angry at me? My blood simmers. That's rich. If this is how this weekend is going to go, so be it.

Chapter Thirty-Four

Jo

"**I** AM SO HAPPY YOU'RE HERE!" MILDRED SAYS LOUDLY, HER SMILE wide as she stretches her arms open to hug my mom.

Mildred and Roberto Cruz are the quintessential sports power couple. Mildred was a track runner in the Dominican Republic, who won a medal in the Olympics. Roberto was a baseball player who was discovered by the Braves when he was just fourteen years old. I don't know their entire story on how they immigrated here, but I've heard enough immigrant stories to know it couldn't have been easy, even with a major league team facilitating it. Leaving family behind and moving to a foreign country could never be easy. My family has been here since my grandparents moved to Raleigh and both of my parents were born here, so I can't relate to what the Cruzes have been through. Not that they're crying about it. Roberto is a hall of famer who signed multimillion-dollar contracts with sponsors and Mildred hung up her cleats early on to become a journalist and is now the founder and CEO of a magazine that rivals the best of them. When I asked her why she decided to go that route she said her goal was to put more marginalized people on magazine covers. It's not just a sports magazine, but a lifestyle brand that she's built from it. It's safe to say that they're living the American dream. Mildred, who has her hair up in a sleek high ponytail, walks over to Misty first, hugging her tightly and smiling wide, and then me, doing the same.

She has long arms like her sons', which is why it's no surprise that they're all so tall, with one parent who's well over six feet and another who's right on the cusp of it. Mildred could have been a model, with her height, thin frame, olive complexion, and bright green eyes. She small talks with us outside before welcoming us inside her home, which is stunning. I'd been there when I was young, but that was before they remodeled the place. Now it looks very much like a modern-day farmhouse, sleek yet classic, with neutral tones and open spaces. What makes it stunning, though, is the view. The back of the house overlooks the mountains, and the entire thing is made of glass, so it's all you see. I stand there for a long moment, admiring the beauty, until Jagger and Maverick's deep chuckles pull me out of my reverie. When I turn around, I see them both hugging their mom and letting her kiss their cheeks. I might hate Jagger, but I feel my lips tug into a small smile at the sight. Most guys our age are quick to dismiss affection from their parents. Not these guys though. I'd forgotten what a tightly knit family they are until now. Always together, never arguing in front of people, never going against what their mother tells them. I sit with that for a moment. Me, who completely goes against everything her parents say because I always think my ideas are better.

"Welcome, *familia*," Roberto boasts as he walks in the door with some grocery bags in his hands. "I tried to go get some wine before your arrival, but you beat me back here."

"I was desperate to escape Cary," Dad says, smiling as he greets his friend with a quick hug and pat on the shoulder.

"Why don't I show you to your room?" Mildred asks Misty and me. "That way you can make yourselves at home."

I pick up my bag and my sister rolls her suitcase as we follow Mildred and my mother, who are walking ahead of us, talking about the décor.

"Rosa tells me you're studying journalism." Mildred looks over her shoulder at Misty. "You know I'm going to want you working for the magazine."

"I would absolutely love to," Misty says, smiling. "New York is always calling my name."

"I'm glad to hear it."

"That makes one of us," Mom says. "I've been enjoying having her back home, even if she did refuse to come back to the house and was dead set on having her own apartment."

"I go home every weekend," Misty says.

"At least one of you does." Mom shoots me a look, then smiles. "Though I'm hoping Jo will join us for dinner on Sundays from now on."

"I will. As soon as I get my car working." I let out a laugh.

"I spoke to your father about that. I think you'll find that you'll have a working car again soon." Mom winks. Misty reaches for my hand and squeezes, letting out a little excited squeal. I laugh.

"Here we are." Mildred steps inside a bedroom that has the same view as the living room, enormous windows that showcase the mountains. There are two queen-size beds with white comforters and a large television on the opposite wall. It looks like a spa. It even smells like a spa.

"Wow." I step inside and go to the glass door that leads to a balcony.

"The balcony wraps around the house," Mildred says. "The boys' room is next door, but I already told them to be on their best behavior. No walking around naked or half naked, as they like to do."

I'm glad I'm facing forward because I feel a blush come over me as I think about Jagger walking around half naked in the house we share. *The house no one knows we share.* The house we may no longer be sharing soon enough if we keep this up.

"I know you girls like to explore, so if you want to go shopping or whatever, there's a car at your disposal," Mildred says. "The keys are hanging by the garage door."

"Thank you," I say.

"You're too kind, Milly," Misty adds.

"Nonsense. You're family." Mildred waves us off. "Come, Rosa. Let me show you to your room."

They shut the door behind them when they leave and Misty and I sit in our respective beds. We always choose sides—her bed is always the one closest to the bathroom, so mine is naturally the one closer to the window.

"It's really beautiful here." I smile as I look out there again.

"It really is." She sighs, plopping back onto the bed. "So comfortable too."

I pick up the control beside me on the nightstand and examine it. I click a button and the window turns dark. I click the other one and it goes back to normal. Cool.

"Are you going to talk to Jagger?" Misty turns onto her side.

"Nope."

"That's fair." Misty nods. "I mean, it'll be difficult to avoid him this weekend, but I respect that decision. He's still a dick."

"He is." I shut my eyes and face down on the bed.

I've been trying so hard not to replay that video in my head—that girl straddling and making out with him, and according to my sister, disappearing upstairs with him. Every time I think about it, it feels like another punch in the gut. He was so quick to judge Lawrence for his infidelity, so quick to tell me all about it and warn me against him, and yet, this is what he does once he earns my trust? No, we weren't together the way Lawrence and I were, but still. It's still messed up. It still makes me sad and mad and like I want to punch something, preferably his gorgeous face. But I won't.

I won't.

Chapter Thirty-Five

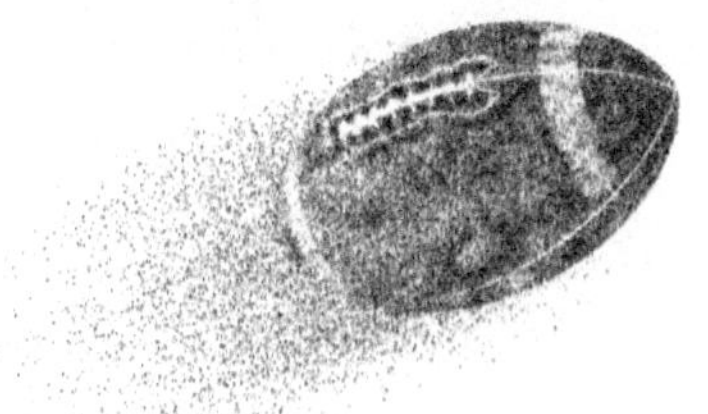

Jagger

MY BROTHER HASN'T STOPPED TALKING ABOUT A BREWERY HE wants to visit, so finally, after dinner, I get ready and take him up on the offer. Anything is better than sitting around this house with Jo so close yet so far. Not that I want anything to do with her. My head and heart are at odds with this though. Or maybe it's my dick and my head. I'm not quite sure. All I know is that when she walked out of her room wearing those tight jeans and that black bodysuit that dips so low that's just begging for me to reach out and lower it even more, to let her perky breasts loose and suck her pretty nipples into my mouth, I knew I had to bolt out of there. It's bad enough she went back to that dickhead Lawrence. I definitely don't need the reminder. I haven't even been home in a week because I knew seeing her would bring out something in me that I wasn't quite ready to expose. It would be ugly. I thought having the week away from her meant that when I saw her again I'd have control of myself, but I was wrong, because the moment I saw her at her parents' house I wanted to grab her by the neck and fuck her. I'm sick. I must be sick.

"You're not going to invite Misty and Jo?" Mom asks in the kitchen, when we're out of earshot from everyone.

"Nope. Boys' night." I grab one of the crackers she's serving on a charcuterie board and shove it into my mouth.

"Make it a girls' and boys' night." She slaps my hand when I go for another cracker.

"I don't want to."

"Why not?" She stops messing with the cheeses and looks at me. "You need to learn to be a good host. You can't just disappear into the night." She stops talking when Misty walks into the kitchen. She's wearing a short flowy dress with a flower print on it and sandals. "You look nice," Mom says.

"Thanks." Misty smiles wide. "We're going out."

"Oh." Mom raises an eyebrow, then looks at me quickly. "Jagger and Maverick are planning to go out as well. Maybe you can all go together."

"Hm." Misty sets her lips flat, looking over at me and there's no mistaking the anger in her eyes. It takes me aback, because what the fuck? Her sister is the one who screwed me over, not the other way around. "I think we'll have to pass. You guys have fun though."

"You too," I say, then scowl when Jo walks into the kitchen, those jeans too tight, that bodysuit too provocative. "What are you so dressed up for?"

"You call this dressed up?" Jo shoots me a look. "Misty's wearing an actual dress."

"You're both dressed up," I say.

"You both look great," Mom says, winking. She shoots me a *what is wrong with you?* look before picking up the tray and walking out of the kitchen.

"You're dressed up too," Misty points out.

"I'm not." I'm really not. I'm wearing jeans and a red polo.

"Well, if you must know, we're meeting some guys up for drinks," Misty says. My gaze shoots to Jo, who bites her lip and looks away.

"What guys?"

"Guys you don't know," Misty says. "You think you know everyone in this town too?"

"How do you know anyone in this town?"

"Because I freaking do and again, it's none of your business what we do." Misty places a hand on her hip. "Have fun. We know we will."

They grab two bottles of water and walk out of the kitchen and soon I hear the door open and a car pull away.

"You ready to go?" Mav walks into the kitchen wearing jeans and some kind of Manga T-shirt.

"Yeah."

"Did you invite the girls to come with?"

"They already left. Apparently they're meeting up with some guys."

My brother raises an eyebrow. "Lawrence?"

"I don't know." My blood starts boiling.

Asheville is small enough that we may run into them tonight and if we do and she's with Lawrence I need to know I can handle it because otherwise I'll break his face. I decide I'm sticking to two beers tonight. It's the only way I can ensure keeping my wits about me and not letting my emotions control the situation. I say a version of this to my brother as we walk outside and get in one of my dad's cars.

"First of all, you're assuming too much. We probably won't see them. Secondly, did you see how she looks in that outfit? I feel like drunk or not, if you see her with anyone tonight you're going to flip out. Third of all, this is on you for not telling her how you felt."

"I didn't get a chance to tell her how I felt." I glance at him as we wind down the hill and onto the street. "The night I was going to tell her, she got back with Lawrence."

"Did you ask her about that?"

"I didn't have to. You were there. You saw them."

"Did you text her to confirm this?"

"Can you not?" I shoot him a look.

"I'm just saying, Jag. You've liked this girl for as long as I can remember. Sure, you had other girlfriends and other people you were fucking, but Jo has always been your *if she ever gives me a chance I'll change full-stop* girl. She gave you a chance, finally, and then you just . . . let him have her back?"

"That's not what happened." I frown. "We were casually hooking up, at her request."

"Her request, Jagger?" My brother turns to me as I finish

parallel parking near the brewery. "You're the king of casual. How is she supposed to think this would be anything but that?"

"How is it that you still don't have a girlfriend?"

Mav chuckles. "That's by choice and when I do get one, I'm not going to be playing all of these stupid mind games."

"Famous last words." I raise an eyebrow.

We take a seat and order our beer. Mav orders a flight and I order one of the ones they have on tap. There's a game on, but it goes to halftime and they start showing the reel of last week's highlights, talking about me again. I keep my eyes on the television and read the caption since it's loud in here. They're still praising the play. Most of them praised it. Some of them criticized how risky it was. Coach said the same thing after all of the celebrating was over. It was risky, especially since it was early on in the game, but I do that. I take risks. On the field, that is. Before I catch myself, I take my phone out and text message Josephine.

Chapter Thirty-Six

Jo

GLANCE DOWN AT MY PHONE AND FREEZE WHEN I SEE THAT MY incoming text is from Jagger. I look around quickly, thinking maybe he spotted me, maybe he's here, but I don't see him anywhere, and I would and not just because my skin prickles whenever he's near. Maverick is hard to miss, tall, all roped in muscle with that mean gleam about him that he has, which is funny since he's a sweetheart, but you'd never know it. I open the text and read it.

We need to talk.

I let out a laugh, clicking the side button before turning my phone over so that I don't see the screen. Misty shoots me a questioning look, and I shake my head to dismiss it. She wasn't lying when she said we were meeting up with some guys. What she failed to leave out was that Eric has been our good friend since we were kids and he and Paul are a couple. They're both hot as hell though and have been known to pretend they're our boyfriends when we go out and don't want attention from guys.

"Trouble in paradise?" Eric asks, raising a brow.

"It was never paradise, only trouble."

"Your favorite kind of vibe," Paul says across the table. We all laugh. "I will say, it's about damn time you left Lawrence."

"I'll drink to that," Eric says beside me.

We all clink glasses and take a sip of beer.

"I didn't realize y'all hated him so much." I frown.

"Really, Jo?" Eric shakes his head. "The guy was the ultimate douche."

"No, he wasn't." My frown deepens. "I mean, sure he was a little arrogant, but he wasn't mean."

"He was mean," Paul says. "But let's move on. We're done with him anyway."

"So, Jagger Cruz," Eric muses. "He's the oldest of the trio, right?"

"Yes, and he's a Gemini," I say. "Since I know that's your follow-up question."

Eric chuckles, running a hand through his perfectly bleach-blond hair. Normally, that look doesn't do it for me, but with his spray tan and deep blue eyes, the blond hair looks hot. Not that he cares what any of us think. Eric has always been sure of himself and worn his skin rather than letting it wear him. In my insecure phase, I often summoned his confidence, but never achieved his no-fucks-given attitude.

"You're an Aries, so that works," Eric says.

"It's like us, babe," Paul says.

"Let's hope he's not as crazy as you are, honey." Eric sips his beer, eyes twinkling. Paul flashes him his middle finger.

"Tell us about your venture," Misty says. "Are you allowed to grow and distribute? How does this work?"

Eric and Paul put on their business caps and start talking to us about their marijuana company. It's already been approved for medical usage, but not in the state of North Carolina yet. They explain the long, drawn-out process, but the way they talk about it, with such pride, tells me this is one thousand percent what they should be doing. It's a long moment before my phone vibrates again. I'm two beers in at this point, so when I see another text from Jagger, this time saying, *I see you. Meet me in the bathroom. Let's talk.* I don't think twice. I hop off the barstool, holding on to Eric's shoulder to steady myself, and stand up.

"Bathroom?" Eric asks. Misty and Paul are lost in conversation still, so when I nod, Eric stands up and holds my hand. "Let's go."

I don't even stop him or tell him I'm meeting Jagger there. The alcohol went straight to my brain and I feel like I'm swaying on my feet. The restrooms turn out to be a long hall of gender-neutral doors with shared sinks right outside of the doors.

"You good or do you need help?" Eric turns me to face him and looks down at me. "You know I've been to this rodeo before."

"I think I'm okay." I laugh thinking of all the times Eric has helped unzip and re-zip my outfits over the years.

"You're full of surprises." Jagger's voice startles me.

"I'm sure you mean that in the best way." Eric's eyes shoot to Jagger, who's obviously standing behind me.

"Who the hell are you?" Jagger asks.

"I would ask the same, but the fact that you're clearly an asshole just answered my question." Eric's eyes are hard as he assesses Jagger. I finally make myself turn around and God I wish he wasn't so damn attractive and I wish I wasn't so damn attracted to him.

"Can we talk alone or is your newest plaything going to join in on the conversation?" Jagger asks, his jaw twitching.

"I'm not her plaything. I'm her constant. I was here through the last relationship and will be here after you're discarded, so I'd watch my mouth if I were you."

"Really?" Jagger raises an eyebrow. "The plot thickens."

"I'm good," I say, looking up at Eric. I squeeze his hand twice so he knows I mean it.

"Maybe I'll stick around in case I need to bash someone's face in," Eric says, taking his hand from mine and crossing his muscular arms across his chest.

"Maybe you should mind your own fucking business before I make you regret it." Jagger steps forward.

"Stop." I put a hand flat on Jagger's hard chest. His fiery gaze meets mine. "Stop. Now. Or there will be no conversation."

Jagger nods once, twice, jaw still twitching.

"You sure you don't want me to wait for you?" Eric asks.

"I'm sure. Thank you." I smile at him.

"I'll be back in five." He walks away, back to the table.

As soon as he's out of sight, Jagger grabs my arm and walks me into a bathroom, shutting and locking the door behind us.

"What the hell?" I yank my arm from his grasp.

"Explain," he seethes.

"Explain?" I raise an eyebrow. "What exactly do you need me to explain?"

"This is your new casual hookup? Is that what's happening? You got back together with Lawrence and now you're giving him a taste of his own medicine, or is this a mutual agreement you have now?" He crowds my space. I put my hands on his chest so he can't come any closer, but his warmth makes my hands tingle.

"Eric isn't a casual hookup," I say. "Not that it's any of your business after what you did."

"What I did?" He blinks. "What exactly did I do? You were the one who got back together with Lawrence."

"I . . . what?" I let out a laugh. "What the hell are you talking about?"

"Lawrence. I saw you together. I went to the bar after my game because I wanted to see you. I wanted to . . . " He shakes his head, eyes as hard as his chiseled jaw. "It doesn't matter. I saw you leave with him, hold his hand, let him touch you. I have never felt my skin crawl like I did that night."

"No, you just let other women crawl all over you instead." I push his chest. "I saw the video."

"What video?" he looks bewildered.

"The video of you at that party. You were making out with some girl with long, dark hair. Misty was there. She saw you go upstairs with the girl. Holding hands," I grit out. "So don't tell me what it feels like to have your skin crawl. You said we were exclusive. You lied."

"I did not lie. I never so much as looked at another woman while we were together. Why would I?" He searches my gaze, which is as hard as his.

"I don't know, Jagger. Why do men do anything?"

"I did not . . . " He takes a step back, running a hand through his dark hair as he shakes his head.

"Don't bother coming up with any excuses. I know what I saw. My sister knows what she saw."

His gaze snaps to mine again. He walks forward. I take a step back, hitting the wall behind me just as he plants his arms on either side of my head and lowers his face. His voice shakes as he speaks.

"I never slept with anyone else. I did not sleep with that woman."

"Right." I roll my eyes, but my own voice is shaky, and when I take a breath to clear my head, I inhale his scent and I find myself getting drunk off that as well. "I don't believe you."

"I don't give a damn if you don't believe me. It's the truth." He slaps a hand on the wall. I flinch at the sound so close to my ear.

"If you don't care whether or not I believe you, I guess there's nothing more to discuss." I keep my gaze locked on his. "Now, if you'll excuse me, I need to get back to my casual hookup."

I duck underneath his arm, but he straightens and grabs

me again. I pull away once more, but his voice stops me just as I reach for the lock. "I care."

"I don't believe you." I speak to the door in front of me, not wanting to meet his eyes again.

"That night, after my game, I went to the bar to tell you I'm in love with you." His quiet words snake through me, gripping my heart. I turn around to face him. His gaze, still fiery, burns right into me. "I've been in love with you for as long as I can remember, Josephine. I should've said it sooner. I should have said it years ago instead of pushing you away with my lies, but I was scared. I'm still scared." He takes a breath, glancing away briefly before looking at me again. "But I can't pretend anymore. I don't want to. I love you. I didn't sleep with that girl. I couldn't. Not when every time she touched me the only person I could think about was you."

"But you kissed her," I whisper, hating the tears in my eyes. "I saw you kiss her."

He nods, shutting his eyes briefly. "I thought we were over. I thought you wanted him."

"You should have asked." Now it's my turn to step forward, to crowd his space. "You should have texted. You could have called."

"You could have as well."

"I was in pain. I . . . when I saw you kissing her, I felt like I was dying."

"When I saw him touching you, I felt like I was dying." He closes the distance between us, bringing a hand up to my face. "I'm sorry. I'm sorry I hurt you. I never . . . " He shuts his eyes briefly again and swallows. When he opens them, the pain is as clear as the beat of my heart. "I hate knowing that I hurt you."

I swallow, nodding.

"Will you forgive me?" his thumb grazes my cheek, a soft touch beneath his calloused finger.

"I don't know."

"Please, Jo. I swear I will do anything, everything, to show you I'm worthy of you."

"Promises are just words," I whisper. "I've heard so many promises, so many words." I shrug.

"Not from me." He leans in closer, kissing the corners of my eyes, the tip of my nose. "You've never heard them from me." He pulls away. "Please."

I shake my head, tears springing my eyes again, trickling down slowly. I want him so badly it hurts, I want to believe him and forgive him and forget about that video, but I see it playing in my head and I don't know that I can. Even with that thought, I stand on the tips of my toes and kiss his mouth, soft and slow. Even as I question myself and my actions and what this will lead to, I lean into his touch, into his hands as they pull down my bodysuit, arch my back as his mouth finds my nipples. Soon, we're fumbling fingers pulling our pants down and he's hoisting me up against the wall, my back crashing against it as his mouth finds mine again.

"I don't have a condom," he says against my mouth. "Do you?"

"I'm on the pill." I shake my head. "Clean. I checked after . . ." I let my words trail. After Lawrence.

"I've never . . . " He swallows, shutting his eyes as his fingers find my clit and I moan against him. He opens his eyes and looks at me, fingers still moving against my clit. "I've never had sex without a condom."

"We don't have to—"

"I want to." He searches my eyes. "A bathroom at a brewery wasn't what I envisioned for this, but I can't wait another moment . . . " He bites his lip, exhaling heavily as the tip of his cock teases my folds, throbbing against me, once, twice, before he thrusts inside me. I inhale sharply, gripping his shoulders, my head falling back against the tile of the wall.

He digs his fingers under my thighs as he fucks me, hard, fast, slowly, then fast again.

"Fuck. I'm not going to last." He breathes against me, pushing his forehead against mine. "I won't last, Jo."

His words, the lack of restraint in which he says them, makes me come instantly. I bite my lip to keep from screaming, but when he pounds into me harder, growling in that way he does when he's fired up, I find myself coming again and screaming out his name. He spills inside of me, a burst of warm liquid I've never felt like this, and when we both catch our breath and he sets me down ever so slowly, he turns around, gets a paper towel, wets it and brings it back over to me, placing it between my legs, against my throbbing clit.

"I love you, Jo. I mean that." He pins me with his gaze. "You don't have to say it back. You don't have to return the feeling if you don't love me, but I will never stop, and I know words are just words, but mine aren't. I don't say shit I don't mean."

"Like the fact that you wanted casual?" I raise an eyebrow as I wipe myself.

"Well, I had to reel you in somehow." He grins as he gets dressed and waits for me to do the same. "If I'm being honest, I always wanted more than just casual with you. I still do. I always will. The question is, are you willing to give me a chance?"

"I—" The loud pounding on the door cuts off my sentence. My eyes widen. "Everyone out there is going to know what we were doing."

"Who cares?" Jagger shrugs a shoulder. "We're never going to see them again anyway."

I toss the paper towel in the trash and wash my hands before taking a breath and following him out the door. Eric is standing there, looking between us.

"I think it's fair to say she's mine," Jagger says, holding my hand.

Eric laughs. "I think it's fair to say no one speaks for Jo."

"Facts, so let me rephrase that." Jagger's hand tightens around mine. "I think it's fair to say I'm hers completely and I have no plans on letting her go."

"I respect that." Eric nods, taking a step back. "And I think you should meet my boyfriend. He's been dying to meet you since I described you."

"You're joking." Jagger's mouth drops. He glances at me, then at the back of Eric's head, then at me again.

"You know what they say about people who assume things." I smile.

When we get back to the table, I see that Maverick has

joined us and is talking to Paul and Misty. Misty looks over to me, questioning. I shrug, smiling. She still glares at Jagger though. My sister isn't going to let him off the hook easily. Honestly, I'm not sure that I am either, but I am willing to try, and I truly believe him when he says he loves me, and that he's mine. Only time will tell though.

Chapter Thirty-Seven

2 weeks later

"**B**ABE, DON'T YOU THINK IT'S RIDICULOUS THAT YOU KEEP going back to your room for things?"

I unravel the towel I wrapped around my wet hair and look at him. "Why is it ridiculous? It's not like I'm sleeping in my bed anymore. My clothes are in there and these closets are tiny."

"Did you rip up my jersey?" He looks horrified as he looks down at what I'm wearing.

"I didn't rip it up, I . . . distressed it a bit."

"Distressed it a bit," he repeats. "Coach is going to fucking kill me."

"This isn't a game jersey." I look down with a frown. "Oh my God, is it a game jersey?"

"It doesn't matter." He chuckles, shaking his head. "I have

other game jerseys. Luckily we only have two more weeks before the season is over."

"And then the pros will be waiting," I say.

"We'll see."

It's something we've discussed a lot. The question isn't whether or not he'll get an offer. The question is whether or not he'll take it. He's been thinking about the toll it would take on his body and is trying to weigh out his options. Maybe he'll go pro for a year or two and retire early. Maybe he'll pass up on the offer. I personally think he'll take a contract, but I definitely don't see him staying in the game too long. Not with the kind of awareness he has about his body and what it can withstand. I finish tying up the bottom of the jersey. It hits me at my thighs and it's too loose, so I make sure to tighten the knot by my abdomen.

"Where exactly are you going to be sitting?" Jagger's eyes heat as he looks at me.

"I think first row, right behind the bench."

"So when I run back to the sideline, I'll be able to see you." He walks over slowly, flexing his large hand against my waist and tucking his thumb underneath the front of the jersey. "Some would say you're a distraction."

"Hm." I crane my neck and he rewards me with a kiss.

"Have you told your mom about our living arrangement?" He pulls away, but keeps rubbing his thumb against my stomach.

"No." I shiver.

"My parents are going to be at the game."

"So are mine," I say, biting my lip as his thumb moves dangerously close to the waistband of the shorts I'm wearing.

"I want to tell them about us."

"Hm."

"I'm serious." He takes his hand away altogether and I want to argue, but the seriousness in his eyes keeps my lust at bay.

"Let's tell them."

"Everything," he says, then adds, "Well, maybe not everything, but definitely our living arrangement and definitely about our relationship."

"Okay." I nod. "We'll tell them after the game. They keep talking about going to lunch anyway, as if they know we're going to win this game for sure."

"We are."

I laugh. "So sure of yourself."

"I have to be, baby." He kisses the tip of my nose. "Besides, we're playing Duke. No way I'm letting Lawrence score."

"You don't even play defense." I raise an eyebrow at him.

"No, but all my boys are gunning for him." He winks, stepping away to keep getting ready.

"Be nice, Jagger."

"Nice?" He blinks. "I've never claimed to be nice."

"You know what I mean." I shoot him a look. "Don't hurt him."

"It's football, baby, not bowling." He grabs his bag and walks over to me, bringing an arm around me to grab my ass as he pulls me into a long, seductive kiss. When he pulls away, I'm left wanting more. He knows it too. He smirks. "I love you."

"I love you too," I say as he walks away.

"What?" He freezes and turns around, dropping a hand and bringing the bag to the floor with a thump.

"I said I love you too." I start laughing when he charges me, lifting me up so that my legs are around his waist as he buries his head in my neck.

"Say it again," he murmurs against me.

"I love you, Jagger. I really, really love you."

He pulls away and brings one of my hands up to his chest, against his rapidly beating heart. "You have no idea the things you make me feel."

"Yeah?" I smile.

"No idea."

I grind against his hard cock. "I have some idea."

"God." He groans, throwing his head back. "I can't do this right now, but tonight . . . " He looks at me again, heated expression on his face. "Tonight, it's on."

He makes good on his word. Lawrence is sacked four times and Jagger scores two touchdowns. Another one-hander that will absolutely be on the ESPN highlight reel.

"That's my boy," Mildred screams beside me. "Yeah, baby!"

I smile so hard my cheeks hurt. No one has said anything about me wearing his jersey, even though it's clearly too big for me despite my makeshift alterations. When the game is over, Jagger jogs over to us and jumps up to scale the short wall between us. There are a few photographers there, clicking and getting it on film. His mom reaches forward and gives him a kiss on the cheek as his dad and mine fist bump him. Then he looks over at me, those troublemaker eyes of his making it clear what he's about to do. My heart stops as he moves and leans in, grabbing me by the nape of my neck and pulling me in for a kiss. It's not a chaste kiss, either. I taste the salt of his sweat as he shoves his tongue into my mouth and deepens the kiss. Everyone around us falls completely silent. Maybe it's shock, or maybe it's the fact that my heart is beating so uncontrollably that Jagger's mouth on mine is the only thing I can concentrate on. When he pulls away, he gives me one of his lazy, lopsided smiles, and hops off the wall, picking his helmet back up and running in the direction of the lockers.

It takes me a long moment to pull away from the railing and take a deep breath, my body still buzzing from the kiss.

"What. The hell. Was that?" my mother asks, breaking the silence. "Since when?"

"How long has this been going on?" Mildred adds.

"You have a lot of explaining to do," Dad says.

Roberto is the only one laughing, not a low laugh either, he's full-out laughing as if this is the funniest thing that's ever happened. "That kid. That fucking kid," he says, still laughing. "He always did say you were the most beautiful girl in the world."

My attention snaps to him. "Really?"

"Really." He smiles wide. "Damn, Henry, I guess you're not going to get rid of us after all."

My dad laughs. "I still have to give him a stern talk, you know. I have to at least pretend to be threatening."

Our parents chatter the entire way out of the stadium, and the entire ride to the restaurant, and then while we take our seats they're still talking about Jagger and me and asking questions, but they're talking so much and so fast that I don't even think they want an answer from me. When Jagger gets there, everyone in the restaurant starts clapping for him. I shake my head and laugh at the look on his face as he looks around and waves at them. He walks over to us, says hi to everyone, and gives me a chaste kiss on the lips before taking the seat beside me.

"You have a lot of explaining to do," Dad says, looking between us.

Jagger chuckles, taking my hand in his. "In that case, pass the wine."

We tell our parents about our living arrangement, which makes my mother irate. I'm about to accuse her of being judgmental when she tells me she would have been okay with it, but she doesn't like that I kept it from her. We tell them it happened gradually, though I'm not sure that's the case. Jagger barged into my life and infiltrated my thoughts and senses, I don't think there was anything gradual about it. By the end of lunch, our mothers are planning our wedding and I want to hide under a rock.

"I knew this would happen," I say to Jagger.

"What? You thought they'd be this happy about us?"

"I had a feeling." I bite my lip, frowning.

"What?" He searches my eyes. "What's wrong?"

"If we break up . . . " I start.

"Nope."

I laugh. "If we do though, it'll be a disaster."

"Do you really think I'm stupid enough to let you go?" he asks, with a rawness in his voice I haven't heard. "I love you, Josephine, and I want to spend the rest of my life with you. I have a million questions about my future, but you're not one of them."

"Good." I smile. "Because I don't know what I'm going to do after graduation, but I know I want to go wherever you are."

He brings a hand to cup my face and kisses me again, a tender kiss that makes my pulse race.

"Enough with the kissing," Dad says. "I haven't even threatened you yet."

Jagger pulls away with a laugh. "You don't have to threaten me. I know I don't deserve your daughter, but I absolutely plan on making it so that she never questions her choices."

The entire table erupts with excitement and I can't help but laugh. I don't remember the last time I felt this happy, if ever.

Epilogue

Jagger

"Last game of the season." Coach's words take my attention from the laces I'm tying.

"Last game." I try for a smile, but I'm not sure I achieve it. Coach takes pity on me and

taps my shoulder before walking away.

Last game. Those are loaded words. Last game means I'm free to do whatever I want now, officially sign with an agent, get signed by a team, or not. It also means a lot of us will never see the field again. Not like this anyway. Not where we are the stars and all eyes are on all of us at all times. Players are already getting offers from sponsors, from shoes to cars. I heard Lawrence got a good deal with a big company. He's a quarterback though. Those perks are usually reserved for them.

According to Luis, the agent I'm signing with, a lot of teams have been talking about me behind closed doors, saying they'd be lucky to have me on their roster. According to ESPN, there are more than a handful of places I'd fit in. I would love to say I haven't given it any thought, but the truth is that it's the only thing I think about these days.

That and Jo, but Jo is a sure thing and I'm not worried about her. If she wasn't a sure thing she'd be the only thing on my mind.

"Big day." Jordan walks over with a shit-eating grin on his face. "You ready?"

"I'm always ready."

"Really? Cause you look like you're about to throw up." He chuckles. "Don't tell me

you're having second thoughts about this."

"Never. I just want to make sure we beat the fuck out of Duke so that the aftermath is

that much sweeter."

"I'm with you on that." That's Tucker, who's walking over now, helmet in hand. "The

entire defensive line is on notice. We're not letting Pretty Boy make any complete passes today."

"Good." I feel myself smile now.

This is the last time we'll ever play against Duke as the team stands today, and the fact that we get to kick his ass on this day makes me feel twenty times better about it being our final game. Even with that thought and the celebration we have planned for after the fact, the locker room is quiet, the sound of uncertainty and sadness spreading. The only ones who don't seem as affected are the freshman and red shirts, but that's to be expected. I can't blame them for reeling in the opportunity that us being gone will provide for them.

"Coach wants to huddle now," Brett says, jogging over.

The four of us head to the middle of the locker room and stand around Coach, who's holding an iPad and waiting for us to settle down. He starts giving us one of his heartfelt speeches and goes around naming every player and commending them on one thing he loves about them. He does this every season, but I find my throat tightening today because this is the last time I'm ever going to be on the field with these guys. It's the last time a lot of us will be on the field at all. We huddle, arms around each other as Tucker, the team captain, says some more words that make us emotional, and then we're off, running to the field. I make sure to enjoy the cheers, the boos, and every-thing in between. I take it all in. It's the last time I'll feel this kind of love. I've spoken to enough wide receivers in the NFL to know this. Going pro comes with a different kind of respon-sibility, but none feels like this. These guys and this field will always be my home, regardless of where we end up.

We end up beating Duke 56-24. After the game, when

everyone is high-fiving the other team and saying kind words to them, I think about keeping it short with Lawrence, but he pulls me into an unexpected side hug and pats me on the back.

"I'm looking forward to seeing you out in the field in the future," he says. "I know I fucked up our friendship and don't deserve your grace, but there's no bad blood on my part."

"It's not my grace that should concern you." I pull away from him. "You ruined a girl's senior year. She had to give up her sport because of you. If that shit doesn't weigh on your conscience, I don't know what will."

"I know." He swallows. "That's something I will forever be indebted to her for."

"She put you behind her. You don't owe her shit. Do better, bro." I cast him one last hard look before turning to my teammates and jogging toward the sidelines, where my parents and Jo's are. Jo, Misty, Mitchell, and Mav are also there. My teammates run over to where the cheerleaders are, each grabbing a whiteboard that the cheerleaders helped write, and jog over to where I am. After I climb up and say hi to my parents and hers and my brothers, I pull myself up completely until I'm standing right beside Josephine, who throws her arms around me. I'm sweaty, but she doesn't care.

"That game was crazy," she says against my neck. "You did so good, baby."

"Since it's my last game here, I figured I'd make it memorable." I pull away from her and take a step back. Her brows pull in. "We're supposed to pack up our shit and move out of our house by the end of the week, but I can't imagine not living with you. I don't want to wake up and miss you." I get down on one knee and stick my hand behind my back, where Mitch drops the ring box into my hand; when I pull it around me, Jo gasps, her hands covering her mouth. "I know we haven't been together long, but when you know, you know. Josephine Marie Canó, will you marry me?"

"Oh my God." She laughs, then wipes tears from her face as she nods frantically. "Yes."

I slide the ring onto her finger and stand up, cupping her face with both hands and brushing her tears away with my thumbs.

"I love you, Jagger," she whispers against my lips. "This was so unexpected and perfect."

Our family starts cheering for us as we kiss and I realize that even if we hadn't just royally kicked ass this game, I would have won, because there's no competing with Jo.

"Hey, over here!" someone yells from the field. I pull away with a laugh. I'd forgotten about them already. We look over to see my teammates waving signs that spell out, "Will You Marry Me?"

"She said yes," I shout out.

"Dammit, Jag, she was supposed to look at us first," Jordan yells back. "Did she say yes?"

We laugh. I nod. "She said yes!"

My teammates break out into a dance and start shouting congratulations as our families throw their arms around us.

ClaireContrerasbooks.com

Twitter: @ClariCon

Insta: ClaireContreras

Facebook: www.facebook.com/groups/ClaireContrerasBooks

Other Books

The Trouble With Love

Fake Love

The Consequence of Falling

Because You're Mine

Half Truths

The Sinful King

Twisted Circles

Fables & Other Lies

SECOND CHANCE DUET

Then There Was You

My Way Back to You

The Wilde One

The Player